"You're Getting Old, Dan,"

his sister told him. "Old and ornery. You'll end up like Jacob Sellars, a bachelor dying out in the hills alone. His dog wouldn't even stay with him at the end."

"Is there a moral to this story, Else?"

"Daniel Josiah Blaylock, I've been worried about you since you had diaper rash, but I'm getting tired of the job and want to give your reins to another woman. You've let Hannah slip through your fingers for years. And now she's back."

"Don't you have grandchildren who need tending? Or a sick person who needs chicken broth? Mind your own business, Else."

She smiled and patted his hand. "But I am, dear little brother. Try being a little understanding with Hannah. I figure she's the only chance I have for a sister-in-law from you. You evaded giving grandchildren to our dear departed parents, but you are not going to escape me. Just stop snarling, eat your cake and do what I say...."

Dear Reader,

Happy summer reading from all of us at Silhouette Desire! I know you'll enjoy this July's selections as much as I do, starting with a scrumptious *Man of the Month*, Dan Blaylock, hero of Cait London's *Midnight Rider*. This book will send you running to the nearest ranch so you can find a man like this of your very own.

Robin Elliott fans—and there are plenty of you out there—will be thrilled to note that she's made a return to Silhouette Desire with the delightful, suspenseful *Sophie's Attic*. Welcome back, Robin!

And Jackie Merritt, whose heroes are often "back at the ranch," opts for a change of scenery... but no change of excitement... in *Shipwrecked!* Rounding out the month are three books that are simply not to be missed: *Flirting with Trouble* by Cathie Linz, *Princess McGee* by Maura Seger, and *An Unsuitable Man for the Job* by Elizabeth Bevarly. Don't let July go by without reading these books.

So, until next month, go wild with Desire—you'll be glad you did.

Lucia Macro

Senior Editor

CAIT
LONDON
MIDNIGHT RIDER

SILHOUETTE *Desire*®

Published by Silhouette Books New York

America's Publisher of Contemporary Romance

SILHOUETTE BOOKS
300 East 42nd St., New York, N.Y. 10017

MIDNIGHT RIDER

Copyright © 1992 by Lois Kleinsasser

All rights reserved. Except for use in any review, the reproduction or utilization of this work in whole or in part in any form by any electronic, mechanical or other means, now known or hereafter invented, including xerography, photocopying and recording, or in any information storage or retrieval system, is forbidden without the permission of the publisher, Silhouette Books, 300 E. 42nd St., New York, N.Y. 10017

ISBN: 0-373-05726-1

First Silhouette Books printing July 1992

All the characters in this book have no existence outside the imagination of the author and have no relation whatsoever to anyone bearing the same name or names. They are not even distantly inspired by any individual known or unknown to the author, and all incidents are pure invention.

® and ™: Trademarks used with authorization. Trademarks indicated with ® are registered in the United States Patent and Trademark Office, the Canada Trade Mark Office and in other countries.

Printed in the U.S.A.

Books by Cait London

Silhouette Desire

The Loving Season #502
Angel vs. MacLean #593
The Pendragon Virus #611
The Daddy Candidate #641
Midnight Rider #726

CAIT LONDON

lives in the Missouri Ozarks but grew up in Washington and still loves craggy mountains and the Pacific Coast. She's a full-time secretary, a history buff and an avid reader who knows her way around computers. She grew up painting landscapes and wildlife—but is now committed to writing and enjoying her three creative daughters. Cait has big plans for her future—learning to fish, taking short trips for research and meeting people. She also writes as Cait Logan and has won the *Romantic Times* Best New Romance Writer award for 1986.

To Valerie, who is making my dreams come true

One

On a knoll overlooking the Ferguson ranch house, Dan Blaylock shifted in his saddle. Watching the woman in the shadows of the porch, he eased aside his denim jacket and gently probed the bloody handkerchief covering the gash across his ribs.

At the midnight hour, he felt as ornery as the young bull he'd been chasing. El Capitan, a descendant of the famous Texas longhorn, had ignored barbed-wire fencing as if it were a weak spiderweb and had happily pursued his lady-loves. The amorous longhorn hadn't wanted to leave lower Wyoming's sprawling fields for the fences of Dan's ranch.

The early November moon slid across the Rocky Mountain night like a gambler's silver dollar rolling across black velvet. Dan tracked the woman moving across the old porch. Hannah Ferguson Jordan had come back to his lair and this time they'd settle the past between them. She'd gotten away too easily sixteen years ago. But now Dan held the reins of her life in his fist; before Hannah flew out of his reach this time, she'd pay him back.

Catching the moonlight, her long white robe shimmered in shadows. She leaned against a supporting post and looked up at the sky.

Under the cloth, her skin would be soft and warm, he thought fleetingly, fighting the pain in his side and the cold night. His hand pressed the ragged wound crossing his ribs and his mouth tightened against the pain.

He concentrated on the long hair sliding down her breasts, shadowing them. Those who remembered Hannah Ferguson said her dark red hair signaled a pepper-hot temper that only Dan seemed to rile. When he came near her, they said, she'd ignite into a hellcat.

"Smokey," he murmured rawly, the sound of his voice catching in his throat and drifting away into the pines surrounding him. Dan ran the back of his hand across his forehead, not surprised at the cold sweat and the feverish heat of his body. He'd lost blood, his chambray shirt sticky with it. But nothing could keep him from her tonight.

God, how he wanted her. Maybe it was the effect of the pain pills on the heels of a hangover, but he wanted her now.

His thumb stroked the leather reins as he thought of her smooth, warm skin and silky long hair. At nineteen, Hannah's hair had been the color of dark copper, a thick, curling mass that he'd longed to crush in his fists.

But the Fergusons had trusted him with their baby girl back then. The spoiled only child of doting parents and the beloved niece of Earl Ferguson, Hannah had openly resented the way Earl and John Ferguson had trusted Dan.

From the time she was sixteen until she ran away at nineteen, Hannah had been Dan's personal headache. While she'd twisted every male in the county around her finger, Hannah's gray eyes had openly challenged Dan. She wasn't sweet; her flash-fire temper and smart mouth had scalded the boys her age if they stepped out of line.

Dan allowed his lips to curve in a tight smile. Miss Hannah Ferguson had openly stalked him, letting the whole county know that she had set her sights on him.

He grimaced, aching with the pain in his side and the longing to have Hannah's soft, warm body in his arms.

He'd held her off back then, realizing that she was too young for a fair relationship. Drenched in youthful arrogance, he'd decided to let Miss Hannah bridge the six years between their ages. After she'd had a taste of the world beyond Jasmine and the valley, he'd planned to make her his wife. When any young tomcat started making noises about Hannah, Dan had been around to clean up loose talk between the boys. He'd planned to make long, slow love to her that first time, and ground his teeth thinking of any experience she might gain away from him.

He had visions of Hannah in her lacy white wedding gown. Visions of her snuggled against him in the night, drowsy with lovemaking. Visions of her with his children....

That was years ago. Tonight, sixteen years later, he didn't feel like guiding her carefully through any more years as her Dutch uncle. Nor easing back into her life.

He wanted to tear into her world as she had torn his apart.

Because he'd tried to patch himself together in the arms of other women. Because he'd failed.

Her smoke-colored eyes, warm and welcoming when they weren't flashing fire, had haunted him for years. She'd had the sexy look of a woman waiting for a man to touch her.

Nothing but the teary pain streaking her pale face could have reined him that last night.

Nothing.

She owed him, he thought darkly as Durango, his Arabian stallion, shifted restlessly and the leather saddle creaked. She'd cost him sixteen years of unrest, and for dreams and hunger that no other woman could satisfy. She'd knifed a chunk out of his life with nothing to fill in the spaces.

There was no one shielding her now. Not the Fergusons, nor a husband or a child. She'd been on the run, but now she was back in his territory.

He grimaced as pain coursed through him, despite the tablets he'd taken earlier. Nudging Durango with his boot, Dan allowed the horse to pick his footing on the rocky trail down to the house.

* * *

Hannah turned down the damper on the wood stove, allowing the fire to burn slowly throughout what was left of the night. She should be sleeping, exhausted by the two days' drive from Seattle. But the past was waiting to unravel and wouldn't let her rest.

Stripping away the satin robe and tossing it onto a worn rocking chair, she stood in her long thermal underwear and listened to the sounds of the old house fighting the wind. Clinging to her tightly, the long-sleeved top and full-length pants were practical last-minute purchases, as were the workmen's socks covering her feet.

She rubbed the rough fabric covering her arms and stared at the fire dancing in the old stove. At thirty-five she felt old and empty, as though she'd lived three lives and lost a piece of herself each time.

A pine knot saturated in pitch caught fire and a series of tiny sparks erupted in the old cast-iron heating stove. Hannah wrapped her arms around her breasts. She watched the dancing fire, feeling it touch her body—but not the coldness lodged in her heart.

Trapped in fears of the past and the ominous darkness of the night, Hannah shivered and wondered if cornered animals felt the same.

A chipmunk or a squirrel scurried across the porch and the wind whisked a pine bough against the wooden roof shingles.

The past swirled around Hannah as she stared at the flames. Years ago, Hannah's mother, Iris, must have stood before a midnight fire. Unmarried and in love with a married man, Iris must have feared for her unborn child; she would have feared the stigma of her pregnancy and worried about the reputation of Hannah's natural father, Earl Ferguson.

Hannah glanced at the spartan room, the single bed she'd pulled near the heat of the fire and the bucket of water she'd carried from the creek. The old ranch house, the original home of Ferguson settlers, loomed around her, tugging at her memories. Boards or shutters covered the curtainless windows. The electricity had been turned off, and in his later years her uncle—her father, she corrected—had spurned the use of a telephone. When she arrived in the early afternoon, she found the front door barricaded by tumbleweeds. She had managed to clean the main room, which contained the heat stove. The remainder of the house she would clean methodically, sifting through old papers and photographs, scrubbing the wood cookstove and repairing the chimney pipe.

Earl Ferguson had completely swept away any memory of his invalid wife; the neatly kept two-bedroom log home that Hannah remembered badly needed repair. The old barn and outbuildings were in the same condition, the hay bins empty. The attorney who'd contacted her had mentioned that Earl's lingering illness hadn't allowed him to work his beloved ranch and repairs were needed.

Earl had tagged her inheritance with a neat little price tag: she had to stay on the ranch one full year, maintaining it and the livestock, or Daniel Josiah Blaylock received "full legal ownership." During her year of trial, Dan would act as a watchdog, "a single person and experienced cattleman, acting as final council in matters affecting the successful management of the ranch."

Hannah gazed at the fire and frowned. Daniel Josiah Blaylock's big leather glove wasn't touching the Ferguson ranch title.

"Dan." Sliding in a whisper across her lips, the name was a curse she'd never forget.

Tall and lean, looking like the Westerner he was, Daniel Blaylock had been stalked by a continuous flow of beautiful, exciting women. "All Blaylock—part Apache and Spanish mix on his father's side," they'd whispered about Dan's dark skin and black eyes and hair. The middle child of seven Blaylock offspring, Dan had struggled to build his small ranch adjoining Earl Ferguson's larger spread. While Hannah raced through life, there was one male who was immune to her charms—Dan, who regarded her as a child, not a woman.

She'd thrown herself at Dan that last night, after discovering that Earl Ferguson was her father. She'd wanted Dan to soothe her scarred heart as he always had. Finding him wrapped in the steam of his shower and the arms of Bernadette Finley hadn't been soothing. Neither had the discovery that for years he'd known Earl was her father.

Bernadette had slipped away sometime during the furious argument and before Hannah had thrown a black pottery vase at Dan's arrogant head.

Something had snapped then, as Dan gathered her roughly against him for the first time.

Dressed only in hastily donned jeans, Dan had forced her face up to his and pressed her against the hard, demanding thrust of his thighs.

She'd never forget his rough, hungry kiss, nor his anger and contempt as he pushed her aside. "Grow up," he clipped out, then ordered her to go home.

"You're not telling me what to do! Ever, Daniel Blaylock," she'd managed shakily.

"Smokey," he'd rasped huskily, staring down at her tender, swollen mouth as though he'd like to devour it, "There will come a time... Back off before we're both sorry."

An hour later, she'd taken what cash she could find, slammed her red Corvette into gear, and had roared out of town in a cloud of dust.

Now Hannah ran her palms up and down her arms, warming them as the mountain wind howled around the house. A wooden shingle tore free in the wind, rolling down the steep roof and clattering on the porch. She inhaled, fighting the loneliness surrounding her.

She'd been wrong to run away sixteen years ago. She'd been wrong to hate for so long.

Five years had slipped by, nibbling at her pride while she'd gone to college. John Ferguson, the man she thought was her father until that blinding night of pain, had died, and she'd been busy fighting for a career in interior decorating. Another three years passed and she'd married Ethan Jordan on a lonesome whim.

Exchanging information bits about her life for Earl's letters yielded an ache for home and a bitter pain. Time became a trench and she found excuses to maintain the distance.

In five years of marriage, Hannah and Ethan built Jordan Interior Design into a moderately successful business. In the two years it took Ethan to buy out her interest after the divorce, Hannah continued working feverishly and tried to sort out the tangle of her life.

When Earl passed away, she knew her survival depended on placing the past at rest.

Packing her vintage white Volkswagen with necessities, she'd taken a last breath of Seattle's salty air and headed toward Wyoming.

Hannah frowned as another pine knot caught fire. She'd been spoiled and hurt, discovering that Earl Ferguson was not her uncle, but her father. Hugging herself, she ached for all of them. For John Ferguson who married Iris when she became pregnant with Earl's child. For Iris who loved both men in different ways.

For teenage Hannah, torn by the painful discovery and spiteful in her pain.

Aching with the past, Hannah shivered as the cold wind, coming from the open door, slammed into her.

"Smokey?" Dan Blaylock's drawl shattered the fragile memories and the quiet night as he kicked the door shut.

"You!" She reached for her robe, holding it against her breasts.

"That's quite some getup," he said huskily, tracing the tight, revealing underwear. In the light of the wood stove, Dan grinned, his teeth showing whitely against his dark face and beard. His worn Stetson was tipped back from his face, his black hair whipped by the November wind. The firelight danced across his dark face, catching on the high cheekbones and slashing eyebrows. Daniel Blaylock had never been pretty-boy handsome, his rugged features too strong, and now the years had given him a dangerous look. Or was it the night and her emotions?

Beneath a broad forehead, lashed with strands of straight, sleek jet-black hair, his dark eyes—Spanish eyes, locals called them—traced her face. The best tracker in the countryside, Daniel Blaylock had once searched out a lost child with those eyes, just as he now tracked her shattered emotions.

Hannah forced her chin up, returning the scrutiny without flinching. Dark and weathered, the lines deeper now, his skin reflected his Native American heritage. Tracing the uneven bridge of his nose, she remembered the tavern brawl that had broken it. His hard mouth curled now with amusement as she determinedly faced him. Beneath the black stubble of his beard, a tense muscle moved slowly, rhythmically, in his rugged jaw.

Dressed in a worn denim jacket, jeans and leather chaps, Dan Blaylock hadn't lost a dram of his sex appeal. His grin widened as his black eyes stroked her body, lingering on her legs. "Why, I do declare, Miss Hannah Ferguson at her pale-skinned very best," he drawled in a deep tone that sent her nerves scrambling.

"It's Hannah Jordan now," she corrected, firing the words back at him. She'd found a moment's peace to reckon with the past and Dan Blaylock stepped boldly into it. "Stop leering. You could turn your back while I put on my robe," Hannah managed through her teeth. She was trembling, fighting the reaction of seeing the man who had stalked her dreams through the years.

He'd called her a pale-skinned princess back then.... And Smokey.

His lifted eyebrow mocked her. "Modesty? This from Hannah Ferguson, who delighted in shocking the valley with her bikinis and short-shorts?" He glanced at the lacy bra tossed across her suitcase and the washcloth and enamel bowl on the table. Hannah's fingers crushed the satin robe; she didn't like him tracking her when she wasn't prepared.

"Dan, get out. You can toss your weight around tomorrow. Make an appointment," she ordered tightly as another sliver of wood burst into flame.

"Tomorrow will have to take care of itself," he returned slowly as his expression stilled. His dark eyes flickered down her once more before he walked to her.

In his boots, Dan was almost a head taller than her five-foot-nine body. Scents of wood smoke, pine and leather clung to him with the cold November air. "So you came back after all," he said softly as though repeating his thoughts aloud.

"I didn't have a choice, did I?" she returned, refusing to move away from him as he studied her upturned face. She could meet him on any level now, not a half-grown wounded girl pitted against a man who thought she was amusing at best.

"You won't make the year Earl set out in his will." The challenge was issued, Dan's dark eyes flickering beneath his long lashes.

She'd thought of his voice as velvet....*Smokey*, he'd said, breathing hard after the hot kiss and his arms tightening possessively around her. And then he'd shoved her away in disgust.

"I can manage a year," she returned evenly, meeting his searching eyes as she tightened her arms around her chest. She intended to manage a lifetime—without Daniel Josiah Blaylock's black eyes prying into her wounds. She was set to dig into her land. "Ferguson land is not defaulting to you."

His hand reached out to stroke away a long tendril from her cheek, then snare a curl and wrap it around his finger. "This isn't Seattle, lady. You'll have to tend Earl's prime buffalo herd and his Herefords. Pitching hay in winter isn't interior decorating."

"Well, damned if it isn't." She smiled coldly, refusing to let him see her reaction to his taunt. She didn't want to shiver, clutching the robe higher, a shield between Dan and herself as he continued studying her face.

His gaze touched her lips and she firmed them to keep them from trembling. "You look tired and thin."

"Thanks for the compliment." She shot the words at him, fighting the tension within her. Dan had chosen the perfect.

hour to step back into her life. His fingers eased beneath her hair, searching for her scalp and rubbing it as though she were a cold, wet kitten who needed comforting.

In the shadows over her, Dan frowned, the firelight glistening on his day's growth of beard. His black eyebrows drew together, his eyes searching hers, tracking the years. Something hard and hot and haunting flickered in the coal-black depths. Something she didn't want to remember when his lips moved slightly. "I could use a stiff drink or a cup of coffee."

"I'm not welcoming you anytime, anywhere, Dan. Get out." Hannah fought from stepping into the safety of his arms the way she'd done years ago. Jeff Morrisey had just totaled his father's truck and she'd climbed out the passenger side to the safety of Dan's welcoming arms. He'd trembled, gathering her closely against his hard length, his lips buried in her tangled hair. He'd lashed at Jeff furiously, a hot blend of Spanish and Western cowboy curses. But all the time, he'd held her closely, soothing her with his hands.

She remembered the hard thud of his heart against her cheek. As though he'd been in the wreck, too, scrambling up the ravine before the vehicle ignited into flames. Leaving Jeff to follow, Dan had carried her to his truck, carefully placed her inside. He'd kept her tucked against him for the entire ride to her parents' ranch.

A dead branch, torn free by the wind, struck the roof, rolling down in a series of thumps as Dan's hand stroked her cheek, leaving a warm path, and for an instant his expression softened. "So you're back," he said quietly as though to himself. "Back, and mad as a hornet about it," he corrected, watching her face. "Getting ready to stir up the town, Miss Hannah?" he taunted softly.

She ignored his reference to the name the gossips used to describe her youthful antics. "I'm not happy about you being my watchdog for a year. Nor the fact that if I default you get Ferguson land. Get your hands off me and *my* land, Dan."

"It's a little late to claim an interest. You haven't been back." At that his expression darkened, and for just an instant his hand tightened around her chin. As though he knew he had the right of possession after all the years.

She fought the rage and the tears trembling within her. "Go to hell."

"Tough talk, lady," he said flatly, running a testing finger down her cheek. "For someone who's been crying."

Hannah jerked her head back. He'd caught her raw and bleeding and she hated him for seeing her pain. "Something got in my eye."

"Uh-huh," he said disbelievingly, and in the bare light she noted for the first time the deep lines of strain on his face and the way one hand pressed against his right side. He inhaled suddenly and closed his eyes for an instant.

Hannah shivered, noting the sweat on his forehead and the sudden pale area around his tightly pressed lips. "Dan, what's wrong?"

When his eyes opened, he smiled grimly. "I'm at your mercy tonight, little one."

Little one. He'd called her that aeons ago, too. When she'd come crying to him with torn hands and knees after being bucked off a pony. "Dan?" she repeated, alarmed by the way his hand moved on his side.

Hannah glanced at the crimson stain spreading on the white handkerchief beneath his dark fingers. "Dan, you're hurt." She reached for his hand, lifting it away from the torn shirt. "Oh, Dan..."

She bent to examine the wound, carefully lifting the material away while he stood quietly. The ten-inch-long tear was not deep, but needed stitches. She probed his dark skin gently and was surprised to find it fever hot. "Dan, you need a doctor."

"In the morning." His deep voice was too quiet and she glanced up to find his gaze locked to her breasts. Her heart stopped as Dan's eyes slowly trailed to her hot face.

"Dan..." She'd never seen hunger so urgent in a man's expression, his eyes burning over his high cheekbones. "You're running a fever..." Her sentence trailed away into the night as his large hand fitted over her breast and his mouth sought hers tenderly.

"You came back," he whispered unevenly against her lips, his fingers gently caressing the tip of her breast until it formed a hard nub. Tangled in her rising needs and fighting the warmth of his palm, Hannah started to protest, only to find Dan's mouth brushing lightly across hers, stilling her.

While Hannah fought the sensations racing through her, Dan's lips brushed her cheeks, his breath coming unevenly. "I need you Smokey," he whispered rawly.

The bald statement lashed at her, stunning her until she decided that in his pain Dan must have wanted another woman. Hannah shivered, stepping back and thrusting out her hand. He caught it, bringing the palm up to his lips. Against her flesh, his face was burning hot, his beard rough. Taking his time, Dan nibbled on the soft center, not allowing her to draw free. "Dan, you need a doctor," she repeated, aware of his strength when she tried to step back.

Without hurting her, Dan held her hand easily, suckling one finger at a time. "What do you need? What will hold you? When will you run away again?" The low tone of his voice was an aching caress, sliding lightly over her skin like the tip of a dove's feather.

Hannah stepped back, gripping her robe in front of her. "Dan, I'm taking you to a doctor." She pointed to a chair, suddenly aware of her hand trembling. "You sit down while I get dressed."

When she backed away from him, Dan took one step toward her, his hand pressing against his side. He leaned against a table unsteadily with his other hand and smiled softly at her. "Running away again, Smokey?"

His taunt caught her broadside, reminding her of how she had run from her past. "I'll be right back. You sit down."

Dan's hand lashed out, catching her wrist and bringing her back to him. His thumb caressed the soft delicate skin as he demanded, "You take care of me, you red-haired witch. Cure me."

His eyes were bright, hunger dancing in the dark depths. As though he wanted her.... "Dan, your side needs stitches. You could have an infection now."

His voice lowered, snaring her softly. "So in the morning I'll go to the clinic."

She shook her head, trying to free her wrist. Riding on the knife-edge of painful memories wasn't the time to be near Dan. Yet his eyes held hers in the shadows, the fire crackling behind them. "Take care of me. Let me feel your hands on me.... Just for tonight. Is it so much to ask?"

His fingers released her wrist, sliding free slowly, and Dan stepped back, allowing her the choice. "What are my options?" she asked, rubbing her wrist briskly.

He shrugged, his shoulders wide in the worn denim jacket. "You can say no."

"Some choice," she muttered under her breath, realizing that Dan would leave rather than ask for her help again. She ran her hand through her hair, her fingers trembling as she traced the lines of strain in his face. "You'll let me take you to the clinic tomorrow?"

He nodded slowly, watching her.

"Oh, Lord," she whispered, knowing that Dan Blaylock was hers to take care of until morning. She'd needed more time to fight him, but he stood in front of her now, his lips tight with pain. He was just stubborn enough not to ask again, but to walk out into the night—he'd never make it to town. "I'll probably regret this," she said, placing the huge tin teakettle on the stove to heat water.

"Probably," he agreed, the lines around his eyes deepening with laughter. "But I'm all yours."

The raspy, sensual tone slithered up her spine and she shivered, deciding to keep the situation as clinical as possible. "Okay. Since I'm apparently in charge here, turn around." Dan obeyed slowly, turning to the fire. Glancing at his broad shoulders, Hannah couldn't resist following his taut backside and long legs as she yanked on her robe, tightening the sash with an angry jerk.

Dan stood still as she took his hat from him, placing it on the scarred wooden table over her paperwork. When she drew his jacket carefully from him, he inhaled softly. Blood covered his shirt, seeping slowly through the jagged tear when she removed his hand and the handkerchief. She frowned, scanning his pale face and the lines of fatigue. "I shouldn't have let you talk me into this."

"You're up to it." He shrugged, easing into a rickety chair and watching her. Stretching his legs in front of him, Dan lifted his hand to unbutton his shirt. He grimaced, then sighed tiredly. "Damn, I'm weak as a baby."

Hannah swallowed, then lifted her hands to open his shirt. Dan watched her carefully as she finished the task and unbuttoned his cuffs. Taking care, she eased his left arm free, then the right one. Dan inhaled sharply as she eased the bloody fabric from the T-shirt beneath it, his hand catching on her robe. He crushed the satin folds, his lids closing.

"Hurry," he warned tightly between his teeth.

She allowed him to hold her robe as she cut his T-shirt free, leaving the cloth stuck to his side. Pouring water into the bowl, Hannah dampened the remainder of his shirt and loosened the fabric carefully, aware that Dan watched her, his body taut beneath her touch.

The cotton came free and she dabbed around the wound with a fresh washcloth. A long gash spread across his ribs. She kneeled by his side, probing gently. "Oh, Dan."

"God," he muttered, his hand catching in her hair. "Your hair is still like dark fire." His fingers winnowed through it, lifting it to the firelight as she examined the wound more closely.

When she started to rise, his fist tightened possessively in her hair. "Dan, let me go. I've got a first-aid kit in my car."

As though remembering his wound, he nodded curtly. When she returned, Dan gripped the front of her robe, his eyes closing. Slowly, softly, his dark head lowered to rest on her breasts, his breathing heavy and his face warm with fever. "Hold me. Just hold me," he murmured urgently. "I need you."

Tears burned her lids, her body shaking. As long as she could remember, Dan hadn't needed anyone; she didn't want to think about why she reacted so violently to his touch or his pain. Taking care, she eased his head away and slid her shoulder under his arm. "Come with me."

With an effort, she managed to get him to his feet and the few steps to the metal bed. For a lean man, Dan was heavy, the bedsprings creaking as she eased him to it. He dozed, awakening instantly when she began to dress the wound. "Press the edges together," he ordered, catching the strands of her hair again. "And get me a pain pill from my saddlebags. My horse is outside. Durango will stay put...."

"I'll take care of you and your horse," she soothed, finishing the bandage. "Let go of my hair."

"Damned if I'll let go," he muttered, then sighed slowly a moment later. "Smokey."

After his pain pill and water, Dan slept through the removal of his boots and chaps. As though sensing his owner was in need, Durango allowed her to lead him to a rickety pen and remove his saddle and bridle.

Later, seated beside Dan on the bed, Hannah bathed his face and throat in tepid water. Placing a cool cloth on his forehead, Hannah's fingers trembled as she drew it down his dark, muscled throat and across the corded shoulders. The hair on his broad chest glistened in the firelight, running a vee down to the waistband of his jeans. The white bandage, a contrast to his dark skin, had stopped the bleeding.

Running her hand across her cheek, Hannah shivered. There was no denying the heat moving through her, the heaviness of her breasts and the aching deep within.

She swallowed, watching Dan seek her hand, quieting beneath her touch. Her only sexual experience had been Ethan, who had never evoked a fiery, hungry need. She trembled, fighting the impulse to trace the contours of Dan's lips.

When he'd caressed her breast, Dan's touch had startled her and provoked a reaction that dried her throat and weakened her immediately.

Smokey. The uneven, low whisper tantalized, carrying exotic nuances of sensual magic, long and slow, hot and deep.

He dozed, stirring when she ran her fingers across his damp brow, soothing the sleek black strands touched by gray.

In the firelight, Hannah explored the new lines across his forehead with her fingertips. The dark stubble covering his jaw contrasted with the long, silky lashes sweeping shadows down his cheeks. He turned toward her touch, seeking it, just as her fingertip found a scarred ridge on his right cheek. The scar began just under his high cheekbone and slashed downward into his beard.

Wrapping her arms around herself, Hannah studied him carefully. After sixteen years, at three o'clock in the morning, she ached to move into Dan Blaylock's strong arms.

She eased the covers over him and stood, moving away from him. All she needed now was Dan complicating her single bed.

After wedging two chunks of wood into the stove, Hannah settled down on the rocker. Leaning her head against the back of the chair, she rocked slowly and watched the wood catch fire.

She'd come full circle after a divorce, returning to Earl Ferguson's run-down ranch. And fighting Dan Blaylock after all these years.

Her toe brushed his boot. Oddly comforted by the contact, she rested her foot on it and continued rocking, the rhythmic squeak of the chair reminding her of Earl Ferguson. She remembered the pain in his face when she'd thrown the reality of her birth at him. Tired of fighting the past, she allowed her lids to close.

She dozed, awakened by a horse whinnying outside. Hannah snuggled against the hard warmth running along her side in the old bed. A cow lowed in the distance and she fought the daylight prying at her lids.

"Smokey," a man's deep, drowsy voice murmured against her temple and Hannah's eyes opened wide. A large warm hand caressed her breast, sliding beneath the satin.

She lay quietly, forcing herself not to move as Dan Blaylock's hand slid down her arm. Tangled with his large, lean body, Hannah felt the weight of his arousal pressed against her thigh. Though he slept, Dan's hands and body were slowly, expertly exploring hers, his hand flowing over the curve of her hip, turning, positioning her intimately beside him.

When she stiffened, breathing heavily, Dan's left eye opened. "Don't move. You'll hurt me," he whispered, his mouth resting over hers for just a heartbeat before his light kiss.

"What are you doing?" she demanded hotly, forcing her palms against the steely strength of his shoulders.

Beneath long, silky lashes, his eyes sparkled. "Waiting for you to wake up and take me to the doctor."

She frowned, realizing she was powerless against his strength. "Get off me."

He raised his eyebrows. With his hair tousled and dark eyes warm, Dan didn't look innocent. "Hey. You looked uncomfortable in the chair, so I tucked you in."

"Hah!" Hannah struggled to get her tangled robe from under Dan's leg. He didn't move, continuing to study her until she blushed. "You're not helping."

He grinned rakishly. "Damn right." Watching her carefully, Dan ran a finger down her hot cheek and traced the contour of her mouth. "Temper, temper. You look like you could ignite at any minute, Smokey."

"Why I ever took pity on you..." she gritted between her teeth, suddenly aware that Dan's hand trembled as it cupped her cheek. "Go away."

"Can't." His thigh slid slowly up and down hers, caressing. "You're taking me to the doctor, remember?"

She scowled up at him as he arranged her hair across the pillow with great care. He'd turned slightly, pinning her effectively beneath him, her breasts nudged by his hard chest. "There's nothing like waking up to a hot-natured woman in the morning. Especially one dressed in long johns."

Hannah hadn't let anyone see her defenseless and vulnerable for years. Dan's close inspection had her senses racing and suddenly she felt stripped of all protection against him. "Let me up."

"Sure," he agreed easily, apparently unaffected by her closeness. Dan eased aside, frowning in pain. "Damn."

Slipping from the bed, Hannah adjusted her robe with trembling hands and fought her seething emotions. "I've had enough fun and games."

He eased his legs carefully over the side of the bed and braced himself with his arms. Dressed in boxer shorts, Dan's lean, tanned body caught the light coming from the windows. Cords and muscles tightened as he tentatively touched the bandage on his side. When his hand lifted away, Hannah was startled by the spreading bloody stain. "Dan..."

"Uh-huh, I know," he finished tiredly, the morning light striking his grim, pale face. He looked up, watching her, tracking her emotions again. She resented the close study, the black eyes moving over her face like fingers, searching out the years.

"You'd better get dressed," she said, tossing his clothes to him.

"What about you?" he asked in a low, husky tone that brought her senses scrambling.

Hannah snatched her bra, jeans and sweatshirt from the back of the chair and walked to the door of the bedroom. "I'll dress in the other room.

Minutes later she returned to find Dan dressed in a clean shirt she'd drawn from his saddlebags. He stood near the stove in his stocking feet. Cradling a steaming mug in his hand, he turned to her.

"Ready?" she asked, trying to forget she'd awakened tangled in his arms. Trying to forget how he'd touched her, reverently, his eyes dark with desire.

"I made you a cup of coffee...if that's what you can call it," he offered, nodding to a steaming mug on the table and the jar of instant coffee nearby.

"No, thanks." Hannah shrugged into her jacket. "I'll help you into your boots."

"Now that would be real neighborly," he taunted softly, reaching out to lift her long hair from beneath her jacket and spread it over her shoulders. "Smokey," he added in a drawl a moment later.

His tone reminded her of a cat playing with a mouse.

Two

―――

"No," Dan stated firmly as he braced a dusty boot on the running board of Hannah's Volkswagen. Standing on the passenger side, he glanced contemptuously at the small car. His gloved fingers tightened on the saddlebags resting on his shoulder. "Cute. This toy probably has a name like Pansy."

Leaning against the cold wind, her temper as tumultuous as the gray swirling clouds and mist surrounding the mountains, Hannah jerked open the car door. Digging in the past, Dan stirred it up and served it to her on a platter. Her first car, a used sedan, was named Yolanda and the flashy Corvette's name had been Melissa. She glared up at him. She might not cut him out of her past, but he wasn't making new memories with her. "Maybelle. Take it or leave it, Dan."

Looking all superior Western male, from his worn chaps to his dusty Stetson, Dan lifted his boot from the small running board. His long legs, sheathed in worn jeans, spread wide and locked at the knee. "Not a chance. Get my horse."

"Be sensible, Dan. You're not in shape for a ride across the mountains," she began hotly, holding a long strand of windswept russet hair away from her face.

"You can support me from behind. But I'm not riding in this thing."

Hannah stuffed her hands in her fashionable leather jacket. In the pockets, her fingers curled into fists. "What if I don't help you?" she asked between her teeth. She'd forgotten how angry Dan could make her with that arrogant all-male look.

Dan lifted a black eyebrow, staring down at her coolly. "I'll make it alone. Always have."

"Dan, unless the people in Jasmine have changed, there's nothing they like better than to gossip," she accused hotly, watching his eyes gleam with amusement. The dark beard covering his jaw moved as if he'd smothered a tender smile, the scar shifting slowly.

His eyes flickered, the lines deepening beside them as he swept a finger down her hot cheek. "Why let a little gossip bother you now?"

Hannah brushed his hand away, only to find her hand trapped in his fingers. The stark contrast in pale and dark skin caught her for just a moment and her lips parted. She refused to admit how he still affected her, and looked past him to the pine trees mixed with aspen. "Have it your way, Blaylock. Anything to get you off my property."

Dan's rough thumb ran over her knuckles slowly before he released her. "I intend to have it my way . . . all the way."

When she looked up at him, Dan said softly. "I am sorry about Earl. He was my friend. We got to know each other pretty well."

"Of course," she said tightly, realizing that now wasn't the time to argue about Dan playing overlord to Ferguson land. Nor how he obtained those rights.

Muttering softly to herself, and aware that Dan's gaze tracked the backside of her tight designer jeans, Hannah strode to the barn. Anger rippled through her like lightning zigzagging across dark, cloudy skies. She saddled Durango with quick, efficient motions, surprised at the way her hands remembered the task. Dan had entered her life on his terms, catching her unprepared for those dark, hot eyes staking out each tender nerve and leaving her raw with emotions.

The stallion stood patiently while she adjusted the saddle cinch for a third time. If Dan checked it, he wouldn't find fault. "I didn't come back to play stable boy to Daniel Blaylock," she muttered. There was just something about walking a man's horse to him that smacked of servitude.

Taking a deep breath, Hannah swung up on the Arabian, taking his reins firmly, and allowed him to prance through the gaping space that marked the barn door. The cold wind tore at her hair, lifting and spreading the long strands wildly. The freezing damp mist did nothing to cool her anger when she saw Dan.

He leaned against her VW carelessly, arms folded across his chest. Though the dark Stetson shielded his eyes from her, she sensed his stare as the horse pranced and whinnied. Sidestepping in a fancy show-off, Durango stopped just two feet from Dan's worn boots and Hannah stared down into his black eyes.

"You wanted it. You got it," she stated flatly, then waited for his response. Dan could wait until doomsday before she'd offer to help him up to the saddle.

He lifted his hand slowly to tug down the brim of his hat, a standard Western greeting to a lady.

Dan's eyes slowly stroked every centimeter of her face before moving slowly downward, caressing the length of her denim-clad leg. Lifting higher, his gaze rested momentarily on the rise and fall of her chest beneath the bulky yellow sweater and jacket. Then he looked straight up into her eyes, the look of controlled hunger pushing her breath away. "That was a sight worth the wait. A woman with smoky eyes and the wind catching in that red hair—it's caught what sunlight there is, shimmering like fire now.... A fire woman coming for me," he drawled, drawing a cotton blanket with Indian markings out of his saddlebags.

His tone was dark and low and sensually pagan, ripping through the flip retort on her parted lips. Dan grimaced as he tossed the blanket up to her, then adjusted the bags in front of the saddle. The quick image of his hand resting on her breast the previous night startled her, her fingers tightening on the soft woven blanket.

When his left hand, covered by a worn leather glove, fitted over the saddle horn, Hannah managed to clear her throat. Despite her anger and his taunts, Dan needed her help to survive. Lines of pain etched his dark skin and beads of sweat shone on his cheeks. "Dan, wait. I'll help you...." She began to slide off the horse, only to be stopped by his hand gripping her thigh almost painfully.

"You're not going anywhere, Smokey. Not now," he said quietly, watching her from beneath the shadows of his hat. "Stay where you are."

His eyes locked with hers, and her breath caught in her chest. She saw it then, the raw, shimmering need of a man for a woman, barely shielded by Dan's long sooty lashes. The look, quickly hidden, frightened her as nothing else had for years. Since she was nineteen and he'd branded her with that unforgettable kiss.

"Get behind the saddle. Ride on the skirt," he ordered curtly, not moving until she had reluctantly resettled. Slowly Dan's fingers loosened, his mouth grim with pain and something else. His eyes closed slowly and he took a deep breath before swinging up on the saddle in front of her.

The practiced movement cost him. For a moment he hunched forward, drawing his right arm tightly against his side as though to curb the pain. Then his back straightened slowly, his broad shoulders rigid. His boots found and slid into the stirrups before he breathed quietly. In that moment Hannah found her hand had slipped to his upper arm. Beneath the denim jacket, his muscles tightened. "Dan, this is insane," she began, as his powerful thighs moved in front of hers. He urged Durango toward the mountainous trail that disappeared in the dark stand of fir and red-barked pine.

"The hell it is. Put your arms around me and shut up," he ordered tightly, presenting her with his broad back while settling more comfortably into the saddle.

"You are a hardheaded son of a—" Hannah bit off the last of the curse, remembering Dan's sweet mother. Elizabeth Blaylock had raised seven children and was known for her "heart of gold." She'd taken a wooden spoon to any of her sons who did not open a door for a lady or stand when a woman approached them. Blaylock males were trained from birth to honor a woman's femininity in a courtly manner.

Hannah took a deep breath. "You've got the disposition of a grizzly bear. But that's maligning the bear," she continued hotly. "There's not a chance—"

Dan's big hand found her wrist and guided her arm around his good side to rest on his flat stomach. He inhaled sharply, pressing her fingers against him before shifting the reins into his hand. "You always knew how to sweet-talk a man, Hannah Louise," he said, somehow finding her free hand and placing it on his right thigh.

"Dan!" She resisted, trying to slide her hand on his stomach away and finding it trapped by his arm. His hard thigh moved beneath her fingers, stilling the prancing horse. Dan's hand covered hers, pressing it hard against his leg.

"My right side feels like someone laid a hot poker against it. Keep your hand where it is, Smokey."

Then as though it was an afterthought, Dan lifted her hand to kiss the palm and replace it on his thigh, again covering it with the warmth of his glove. He rubbed it slowly. "When the other one gets cold, slide it under my coat," he ordered, turning in profile to scan the snow-covered mountain peaks.

"That will be the day, Blaylock." Wedging inches between them, Hannah sat very straight and tried to sort out Daniel Blaylock's jarring effects on her. Sitting behind his broad back with her arms around him, her hands warmed by his shifting muscles, wasn't exactly a clinical environment.

Hannah firmed her lips and concentrated on a golden orange aspen leaf carried by the rippling stream near the trail. Dan's disturbing sensuality overpowered the complicated emotions of divorce and guilt.

She closed her eyes against the sight of Dan's blue-black hair fitting over the worn denim collar. As a friend and husband, Ethan was everything she thought she wanted: polished, kind, sharing her interests. They'd worked at their marriage and business with honesty and trust. Yet the marriage failed. *Why?*

Durango whinnied and Hannah opened her eyes to see a red-tailed hawk cut down through the dark gray sky. Turning slightly, she studied Dan's face, contrasting him to Ethan's expensive scent and handsome features.

In profile, Dan's face suited the craggy mountains. A descendant of Spanish conquistadores, Mescalero Apache and white settlers, Dan scanned the wild, rocky scenery shrouded by the low-hanging mist and frost. She traced the scar on his right cheek, following it into the black beard. Daniel Blaylock had the raw, exciting face of a man who caused a woman to think of fire and heat and long, satisfying nights.

Hannah swallowed, trying to forget the way Dan stroked her raw emotions.

"Deer over there..." Dan nodded toward a herd of white-tailed deer grazing in a meadow. "Stop thinking so hard, Smokey. I can almost hear the wheels turning. Put that blanket under you or around you."

"Don't you ever stop giving orders, Dan?" she snapped, realizing suddenly how long it had been since she'd ridden a horse. The muscles in her bottom and thighs had begun to stretch and protest, despite her gym's high-impact aerobic classes.

"Force of habit...I've been taking care of your backside since your folks brought you home from the county hospital."

Hannah breathed quietly, controlling her anger. "When you're feeling better we'll have this out, Dan. I'm a woman now."

He didn't answer, staring at the trail in front of them. "Damn."

Looming in the mist beside the trail, a huge longhorn bull with massive horns stood beside a monstrous buffalo. The longhorn lifted his head, scenting the wind and glorying in his kingdom, while the buffalo bull seemed content to munch on the dried, frosty grass. "I ought to shoot the both of them," Dan muttered darkly. "It's cold up here.... Put on that blanket."

Hannah took a deep breath. "Dan, you're pushing it," she warned between her teeth. Deciding to cut the discussion short, she eased the soft padding beneath her.

"Uh-huh," he agreed, unconcerned, as he stared at the two monstrous bulls. The longhorn lifted his nose higher, outlining his enormous horns against the gray sky. "He's caught my scent. Your scent is confusing him. Between those two, Earl's Hereford cows are likely to throw a mix of buffalo and longhorn. They broke the fence and got to the cows before my bull could."

In an instant the buffalo stopped grazing and tipped his immense, craggy head up to the wind. He sniffed for a moment, then began to snort.

"That's Big Al," Dan stated. "Earl's pet buffalo. He's been showing El Capitan—my young longhorn bull—around the countryside. The tip of that bull's horn is wearing my blood."

"So they're dangerous?" she whispered, leaning closer to him and surprised by the dark red flush suddenly appearing in Dan's dark cheeks.

"They're not kittens, but they're not dangerous if left alone. I was thinking of something else and got careless," he admitted curtly after a long moment.

The animals continued to sniff the wind intently as Durango pranced through the rocky passage, leaving them behind in the mist. In front of her, Dan's big body was rigid.

Somehow the thought of the two animals irritating Dan caused Hannah to smile. Macho Daniel Blaylock might be currently pushing her around, but at the moment he was being challenged. "Unusual pair of friends for you, Dan. Ah...is this a male territorial-rights thing or what?"

Looking down at her across the width of his shoulder, Dan's dark eyes weren't amused. "Did I say something wrong?" Hannah asked innocently.

"Keep pushing, and you're going to find out about male rights," Dan warned, just as a strand of dark red hair caught the wind and slid across his mouth. Hannah captured the strand, sliding it behind her ear, and grinned. Suddenly she felt eighteen, and nothing thrilled her so much as Dan's dark, menacing look. As though with one little nudge, she could send him right over the edge. . . .

"So sorry, Mr. Blaylock," she said primly, wanting to let out the laughter bubbling inside her. There was just something about stroking Dan's nerves the wrong way. Dan deserved a little classical payback.

His glove laced with her bare fingers, his frown less savage. "Same smart mouth. Looks like a long year." His gaze slid down to her mouth, studying the contours until she inhaled suddenly.

"Looks like," she agreed casually, despite her rapidly beating heart. Then to shield emotions Dan's dark gaze had laid open, she added huskily, "You won't get Ferguson land. Not this year. Not the next, Dan. That's a promise."

"Did you love Jordan?" The question slammed into her, hard and hurting.

"You're on the wrong side of the fence, cowboy," she returned with equal force when she could speak.

He stared down at her face, reading and following her hot emotions as though he were hunting...turning over leaf and stone to place his palm on the heat of the ground and what secrets lay uncovered and raw. "Touchy," he murmured softly before shrugging and returning to the trail.

Surrounded by dried meadows and mountain pines, the path was wide and well-worn, showing signs of cattle. "I didn't know there was a trail up here," Hannah said, when Dan continued the silent ride.

He hadn't spoken in a half hour, and in her arms his body had shifted several times. He rode just as ramrod straight, but she noted he favored his side. "Dan? Are you feeling all right?"

Because he wanted her so badly, Dan spoke roughly, "Unless you came along for the pleasure of my company, sit closer. If I fall off, I'll tell Mort Raznick you tried to seduce me in the bushes.''

"Sure," she agreed flatly. "As if I'd want to. Is Mort still around?" she asked, her tone changing to a softer one, drenched with memories. He liked it that way. He liked it any way, he corrected. The years hadn't changed the need to fit his lips over hers and take everything she'd offered back then. "Mort used to have the biggest, fastest mouth in Jasmine...."

"Still does. And yes, I would," he returned smugly, feeling her ease up behind him. Threaded through Durango's reins, his fingers tightened to slow the horse. Dan intended to enjoy every moment of Hannah's body touching his. He closed his eyes, concentrating on her softness pressed against his back. Hannah's tongue might cut like a knife, and she sure as hell didn't like propping him upright, but he needed her. Caught on the silky russet strands teasing his face, her scent snared him as he leaned slightly back against her breasts.

A slashing desire went tearing through him and he closed his eyes, wishing for nothing but Hannah's soft white breasts against his bare skin. For a moment, Durango's slow walking pace reminded him of another slow sensual motion and rhythm...and his body's immediate reaction to her since seeing her again.

"Blackmail," she muttered against his back. "If you weren't sick, I'd leave you for the coyotes. But I'm not fond of poisoning wildlife."

But her hands were on him, just the same, and Dan smiled briefly, despite the growing pain that had begun to shake off the dimming effects of the pill he'd swallowed earlier. "Uh-huh."

Dan allowed himself the luxury of dreaming that Hannah wanted to be exactly where she was...cuddled against his backside, with her arms holding him tight. Momentarily sinking into her softness, Dan allowed Durango to pick his way across the trail toward Jasmine. He must have dozed, sleep dimming the pain slashing his side.

Hannah's arms held him tightly after years of emptiness.

Using his last strength, Dan had forced himself to straighten and grinned as Durango cleared the last stand of trees marking Jasmine's city limits. Smokey clung to him as if she belonged in his life.

At Jasmine's Rural Clinic, eighty-year-old Doc Bennett swore softly as he stitched Dan's side. "Fool thing to do, Dan Blaylock. 'Course I said that the other time you tried to play matador just after Hannah left."

Doc's piercing blue eyes glanced at the scar on Dan's cheek. "Did some fancy stitching to save those pretty looks of yours. Maybe Hannah will have you yet. You got time to have those babies before I retire. Haven't seen a black-haired Blaylock baby come down the chute in about six months."

"Just get on with it," Dan ordered harshly, anxious to find Hannah. She'd disappeared the moment they'd arrived at the clinic.

Dan gritted his teeth. If Hannah walked across the street to the bank—a cold lash of fear snaked through him. Doug Fallcreek was a friend and a good banker, keeping the Ferguson families' accounts private. But Hannah had a right to open the ledgers, and there would be hell to pay when she did.

"The day you were born, I told your mother you were trouble with the ladies." Doc looked over the top of his glasses at Dan's face. "What's wrong, cowboy? Don't you want Hannah to hear how you mooned around for a week after she took off and finally you ended up drunk in a field with a Spanish fighting bull?"

"I was twenty-five, damn it," Dan returned between his teeth, just as another burning stitch went through his side.

"Yeah. Well, Hannah was young and hurt badly. Some pair, the two of you. Too young to have sense and too much pride to bend. You bein' all noble about robbing the cradle. Now, look at you... Forty-one, according to my records. You wasted years, boy. Shoot—"

"Where is she?"

"Hannah?" The doctor examined his finished stitches. "Outside in the parking lot, talking to Addie, my nurse.

Getting instructions on how to take care of you. You need someone to baby you tonight.''

"I've got plenty of family around.'' Dan forced himself upright and the spritely doctor began bandaging him. "If you know what's good for you, you won't say a word about the first time, Doc.''

"Too late. Spouted off the minute you blacked out after the pain shot. And as for any of your sisters or family—we called. You're so ornery when you're sick that none of them claimed to be related. Especially when they heard Miss Hannah was in town.''

"Damn.''

"Made quite the picture, you and her. Riding into town like some cowpoke with his lady on the back of his saddle. High heads, the both of you, shoulders back and filled with pride. Wind whipping her hair around you and you grinning like a loon.''

"That was painkillers, Doc—''

"Sure it was.'' The doctor shook his head and winked. "You looked like one happy hombre—''

A buffalo bull bellowed outside the clinic, matched by a longhorn's loud call. "What's that?''

The doctor's laughter crackled loudly in the sterile room. "El Capitan and Big Al. They followed you into town. You were too high on having your best girl hugging you to notice. Ethel Jackson ran her shiny new Lincoln right into the gully, gawking at them. That's over four thousand pounds of bull standing in the clinic's parking lot, defying the sheriff and cattlemen alike. Hannah's been keeping 'em quiet by talking to 'em while I worked on you.... That's why Addie is outside—mean woman, that Addie, when she gets stirred up. Try to keep women happy when you can, boy.''

The doctor eased Dan into his shirt. After washing his hands, the doctor turned to Dan. "The way I see it is— things are going to get real interesting with Hannah around. The sheriff—your cousin, Mike—is falling all over himself. Just like he did when she won the Miss Jasmine beauty contest in that pink polka-dot bikini and high heels.... He's divorced now, you know.''

Buttoning his shirt, Dan slid off the examining bench and moved to the window overlooking the parking lot. The sheriff's patrol car flashed red lights and a small crowd encircled the scene. Someone had scattered hay on the pavement and El Capitan and Big Al were munching contentedly while Addie and Hannah stood nearby deep in conversation.

Mike moved closer to Hannah and both bulls looked up. El Capitan shook his massive horns. Big Al blew steam through his nostrils. Wiping his hands on a towel, the doctor came to stand beside Dan. "If I didn't know better, I'd say those two bulls were in love with Miss Hannah."

"Crazy," Dan muttered, watching Hannah's hair whip wildly around her head and shoulders. He could feel the warm silk sliding through his fingers, the scent of her drifting on his mind. The softness of her breast weighted his palm again and the smoke color of her eyes ignited...

"Yessiree, Bob," Doc said happily. "That girl always had flash. Miss Hannah is back in town.... There's a whole lot of bull in the parking lot, and a lovesick cowboy standing beside me."

"Send me the bill," Dan said absently, just as Hannah smiled at Mike. The sheriff immediately went into a stance to show off his uniform and sucked in his stomach. She patted his arm briefly, then smiled and waved at Nancy Curtis and several of the people she remembered.... But Hannah was steadily easing her way through the crowd, headed straight for Fallcreek Bank and the Ferguson accounts.

Dan's boots hit the wooden porch of the clinic just as Big Al bellowed. The crowd stepped aside as the buffalo began to sway side to side, lifting his nose to the wind. Big Al bellowed again and began following Hannah's scent toward the bank.

"Dan, your animals are blocking traffic," Mike began as Dan stalked by him.

"Uh-huh," Dan acknowledged. "Watch out for El Capitan's left horn.... It's wearing my blood. Keep the crowd back.... Just let him eat and I'll deal with him later."

"I may confiscate him and that renegade buffalo meat for the town barbecue," Mike threatened hotly, then stopped as Dan slashed a look at him.

"Miss Hannah's back in town," Else Murphy, Dan's older sister, singsonged as he passed.

"Leave me alone and take care of your grandkids.... Make me a berry pie," Dan ordered amicably, knowing that each of his brothers and sisters was just waiting to take potshots at him about Hannah.

"Hi, Uncle Dan," five-year-old Sissy Blaylock called. The youngest of his brother Logan's children, Sissy grinned up at him and pointed her finger to her mouth. "The tooth fairy came last night and I got a quarter. Wanna see where my tooth was?"

"That's nice, rosebud." He paused, lifted Sissy for a quick kiss, then handed her to the safety of her father's arms. Logan Blaylock shifted his daughter to his shoulders and grinned widely at Dan.

"I'll look later, rosebud, okay?" Dan said, stepping around his older brother and Big Al just as Hannah strode out of the bank's doorway.

Without looking, Dan knew exactly what papers were clenched in Hannah's hand. He cursed softly as Hannah struck her thigh with the roll of papers.

"You." Hannah's voice was low and dangerous, her eyes smoky hot in the pale oval of her face as she sighted down on Dan. "You," she repeated louder, the wind whipping her hair into a fiery tempest around her head and shoulders as she strode toward him.

Stepping off the bank's steps and into the highway that served as Jasmine's main street, Hannah stopped in front of Dan. She slapped the papers against his chest, allowing them to fall at his feet.

Doug Fallcreek stepped beside Hannah, shaking his head. "Dan, I..."

"It's not your fault, Doug. Hannah's a mean one when she's riled.... I should have warned you," Dan murmured, watching Hannah's eyes slash at the banker. In a temper, Hannah had never been more beautiful. There was a head-high thoroughbred look about her, like a woman who could take the bad times with the good, bending when she had to and giving as good as she got.

There wasn't an ounce of softness in her right now, with her eyes shooting hot lead and her color high. Dan noted the vein throbbing in her throat, her steamy anger swirling around him.

Her lips quivered, her tongue moving to flick moisture over the soft, full contours. Desire slammed into him with a force he'd never experienced.

A ray of sun shafted down through the rolling clouds, staking them alone in the street as Doug moved cautiously aside.

"I want copies of everything, Doug," Hannah said, spacing her words in a low, husky tone. "A complete accounting for past payments, loans and anything that has sifted through Mr. Blaylock's fingers—including any medical or burial expenses for my uncle."

Her eyes rose slowly up to Dan's. She thrust a vial of pills into his jacket pocket. "Careful how you take those...I don't want anything to happen to you before I get through with you."

The papers at their feet rustled in the wind and Doug quickly scooped them up. He looked from Dan to Hannah uneasily and moved toward the safety of the bank. "I'll have those copied now."

Hannah poked Dan in the chest, glaring up at him. "You and I have business, Mr. Blaylock. Just as soon as I check over my uncle's accounts."

"Take your time," Dan agreed, and decided that at the moment he didn't have a thing to lose by speaking his thoughts. He lowered his voice. "When was the last time you turned all that steam full force on a man?"

Her eyes widened and her cheeks turned pale before coloring again. Dan had the image of something soft and warm and vulnerable, trembling on the edge of pain.

Then, too fast to be concealed, hot rage shot through her and sizzled in the inches separating them before she found her breath. "You don't qualify," Hannah flung back, jabbing him in the chest again with the tip of her finger.

Catching her hand, Dan lifted it to his mouth. He pressed her fingertips to his lips, his eyes locking with hers before she had time to move away. He wanted her to see him coming, to hide nothing of his fierce desire for her. There would be nothing between them but honesty.

The instant stretched into a long, full, breathless moment. Tension shimmered and slid between them so fragile on the mountain wind that the sound of a heartbeat could smash it.

"You are in for hell," she whispered unevenly between the edges of her teeth as she forced her fist down to her side.

Three

___

At midnight Hannah punched her calculator's off button and stared at the files littering the rough table. Dressed in the thermal underwear top, jeans and flat, worn boots, she was exhausted. Her columns of numbers on the yellow legal pad verified that Daniel Josiah Blaylock had indeed fed money into the Camelot. The sums were minimal and deposited when needed. The purchases were baseline, necessary to run the ranch. Payments for Earl's personal needs included a hospital bill.

After the scene on Jasmine's main street, Mike had delivered her back to the Camelot. Within minutes of spreading the papers across the old table, she'd sunk deeper into the reality of Dan's financial control of Ferguson land. Without Dan's management, Earl's estate would have long ago passed into bankruptcy and been sold to the highest bidder on the county courthouse steps.

Hannah snapped the pencil she'd been holding and flung the pieces on her open checkbook, bearing the Fallcreek Bank's crest. She'd managed to do two things before returning to the ranch: transfer her Seattle checking account to Jasmine and persuade the telephone company to connect a line that afternoon. In the morning, she'd call the electric company to reconnect the house. Everything else would have to wait until she knew her budget for the year.

Standing upright slowly, drained by every minute of the past week, she crossed to the window and leaned her forehead against the frosty surface.

In his letters, Earl's shaky handwriting, then another man's stronger scrawl omitted mention of the condition of the ranch and the empty accounts. There were loving descriptions of sprawling fields and new Hereford calves playing amid stacked bales of a lush hay crop. Then there was the underlying whimsy of an ill, elderly man needing his "last surviving relative."

In the window glass, she saw the reflection of a table and remembered another table where two Ferguson brothers sat years ago. At nineteen Hannah had often listened to the low, rumbling voices of her father and uncle and needed that comforting sound after her mother's funeral. Hannah had sat curled beneath her mother's quilt, listening to the men who thought she was asleep.

"Our daughter is just as beautiful as Iris was," John had said quietly.

"You did a fine thing, marrying Iris when she was pregnant with Hannah—my baby," Earl returned after a long moment. *"Neither one of us meant it to happen—"*

Caught by Earl's statement, *Hannah—my baby*, Hannah had listened closely.

"Love comes when it does. I saw you both fight it and lose. I love Hannah as if she were my own. Things worked out, Earl—"

After a pause, Earl stated slowly, *"Iris was a good woman. The gossip would have ripped her apart. When you married her, you saved her reputation. I couldn't leave Margaret then . . . my wife was too ill. . . . There was never anything between Iris and me after your wedding."*

"Nothing but love. Iris deserved that love and respect. She made a good wife and mother."

Hannah closed her eyes, remembering the slicing pain when she discovered that Earl Ferguson was her father.

Why hadn't she come back sooner? Why had she waited to tie her life in Seattle up in neat little boxes with perfect ribbons?

Hannah rubbed her closed eyes. She hadn't cried the drain-me-dry kind of tears since she'd left Jasmine, and wondered if she would again.

One of her neat boxes included cutting her ties with anything that pertained to her marriage and business with Ethan. She'd wanted to manage Ferguson land, repaying Earl for the pain she'd caused. She'd wanted to find what she'd lost through the years, a peace of mind that only the high mountain air and sprawling fields of Wyoming could give her. She'd wanted to do all that without taking her share of the money from the house and business with her. Tangled in guilt and the excitement of returning to the valley, she'd locked the money in an unbreakable five-year trust, taking a few thousand with her to modify or decorate the house to her taste.

Hannah flattened her hand against her stomach to settle it as she glanced around the old house. "Decorate and remodel," she whispered aloud as the towel she'd placed over a drafty window fluttered. "Hardly the right terms. Even the well pump needs replacement."

In the field next to the house, a cow called to her calf and Hannah looked out the window. The moonlight caught on the Herefords' stark white faces.

They looked as though they'd stand there for eternity, waiting for her.

Jerking on her jacket, Hannah left the house to walk toward them.

Steam from their nostrils enveloped the herd, spreading an eerie glow over them as they watched Hannah lean on the fence. "So you're my family now," she said quietly, automatically counting the twenty-five white faces staring at her.

The stocky, beefy lines of each animal stated that they had been well tended, reminding her of Dan's signature on the Ferguson accounts.

Hannah rubbed the forehead of a cow chewing her cud, the warm curling locks comforting as she thought of Dan. "Mr. Daniel Josiah Blaylock, Wyoming cattle king and financier."

Sixteen years hadn't dimmed her need to have him. She didn't want to think about waking up to his touch just hours ago. Nor the way he could make her feel. Whatever had passed in those years, nothing compared to her elemental and shattering emotions concerning Dan.

His hand on her breast had been like a brand, staying on her sensitized flesh long after the moment had passed. The hunger in his eyes had ignited a sensuality she didn't want to discover with him. Dan's vulnerability and pain had struck right through her resistance and the years as though they were spiderwebs before a slashing sword. Hannah closed her eyes, breathing in the warm scents of the earth. She didn't want to hear his softly spoken words, "I need you," running through her brain like a magical litany.

In her lifetime, no one had ever said they needed her.

Wrapping her arms around Dan and supporting him on the back of a horse had proved to be erotic and nerve-shattering. Her hand had rested on his thigh, sensitized to every nuance of hard male muscle sheathed by the worn denim. She'd been forced by the cold to slide her other hand beneath his coat.

Dan's powerful chest had rippled beneath her touch like the sensuous movements of a cat being stroked. Images of his body on her bed, dark and corded with muscle, had simmered in her mind. She'd had to force herself to breathe evenly, totally aware of the rough, hairy texture under the chambray.

Sometime during the hour-long ride, Dan slid his glove off and laced his fingers with hers. His hand had been large, roughly callused and safe.

Hannah's eyes opened wide. "I don't need any of this. Not now," she muttered shakily, realizing that she had been using the board fence for support.

The moment she'd seen his signature in the bank, she'd wanted to fling herself at him, leaving him as bruised as she'd felt. The signature on the papers that transferred money from Blaylock's Flying H spread to Earl's private and business accounts was familiar. Her uncle's last thoughts were written in the same bold scrawl.

Bulky shapes slid out of the pine trees bordering the field. Big Al bellowed, loudly proclaiming his lordly rights over the small buffalo herd that grazed in the moonlight-swept field. "All I have to do is to keep my sanity safe and you prime for a year. Around Dan, that might not be that easy," she admitted slowly, thinking of the bed in the house that still carried his scent.

The telephone rang shrilly, cutting into the peaceful night sounds and stirring of the cattle. She'd turned up the sound on the new wall unit in order to hear it when she worked in the barn lot. Hannah smiled grimly as she walked to the house. Just what she needed—a midnight caller.

Dan's deep voice sank into her with jarring, sexy impact. Spacing his words slowly, carefully, he said, "Smokey, there's Ferguson stock on the Flying H. You come and get him tomorrow noon. Or he's mine."

"You're on painkillers, Dan. Sleep it off and don't call back," she said tightly, while part of her softened and wondered if he'd let anyone take care of him. *I need you.*

"Make that high noon," he said softly after a long moment. "Are you wearing those thermal long johns?"

The line went dead and Hannah stared at the telephone receiver, fury ripping through her like thousand-volt electricity.

Seconds later she had stripped the sheets that reminded her of Dan and lay rolled up in the blanket. If Dan wanted to play showdown, she could handle anything he dished out.

In another moment, she jerked off the thermal top and bottoms and lay shivering in her peach bikini briefs. If Dan thought she wore long johns, she wouldn't. She intended to outthink and outmatch Dan every minute of the next year.

* * *

"Come on, Jessie. Let me in third gear." Hannah shifted the used pickup truck carefully, testing the gears as she drove toward the Flying H adobe-style ranch house. Running her leather glove around the functional scarred wheel, she remembered Doug Fallcreek's daughter sliding into Maybelle's custom seats. Filled with the vivid excitement that had captured Hannah in her teenage years, the girl had grinned up at Hannah. "I'll be very careful with her. Daddy says she's special to you. When you're not so busy, would you teach me how to wash and wax her just right?"

Trading Maybelle for a functional ranch vehicle with cattle racks was the first step to jerking Dan's big leather glove free of Camelot.

"High noon," she muttered, noting the sprawling, well-kept fields of hay and clover and straight fence rows. A series of closely spaced poplar trees created a wind-and-snow break for the unpaved road that lead to Dan's home. Distant snow-covered mountains soared against the clear blue sky.

In contrast to Earl's spread, the Flying H was neat and in good repair. She'd expected expensive improvements, new buildings and feedlots tended by a crew of men. But Dan's ranch looked like a one-man operation, despite the acres of fields and woodlands spreading up to the Rockies.

Adjusting her designer sunglasses against the bright November sun, Hannah noted the enormous rolls of hay for winter feed. A large herd of Herefords spread across a smooth knoll, the rugged mountains rising up in the distance with dark blue arrogance. A barn topped by solar-heating panels blended with the craggy beauty. A beat-up tractor with attached flatbed trailer stood in front of another building, large, gray and weathered. Durango and three other horses grazed in a field of native grass and sagebrush. A prime Hereford bull lifted his broad white face from the feed trough when she stopped the pickup in front of Dan's house.

Another pickup, just as worn as hers and bearing the Flying H, was parked there. Hannah studied the dented

fenders and the dull paint carefully, the image contrasting
with the late model she had pictured. Wherever Dan was
spending his money glut, it wasn't on trucks or his spread.

Hannah's fingers curled tightly around the steering wheel
as she turned her head to the house. It hadn't changed since
the night she'd surprised him in the steaming shower and
Bernadette's clinging arms.

The brilliant sunlight shimmered on the rough adobe
plaster, brushing it with gold and pinks. Dan had restored the
settler's home, enlarging and adding a wide board porch
covered with wooden shingles. Windows lined a south wing
and solar panels glittered on the slanted roof. Though larger
and repaired, the house remained picturesque, nestling into
the pines and soaring, rugged Rockies.

Hannah breathed deeply, forcing her fingers to curl. She
shifted the sacks of groceries and cleaning supplies that had
settled against her and frowned, trying to ignore the stinging pain in her hands. Taking her temper out by cleaning the
dried tumbleweed away from Earl's front porch without
gloves had had disadvantages.

The door handle grated and Dan opened it. Dressed in a
worn flannel shirt, jeans and boots, he looked down at her,
following the lines of her body carefully. He nodded a
greeting. "You always did look good in jeans, Miss Hannah."

Refusing to acknowledge his compliment, Hannah
stepped clear of the pickup. She jerked up her gloves, trying to keep her hands from shaking. "I've come for the
livestock."

He arched an eyebrow, his expression mocking her. "Too
bad. I like the thought of you coming for me."

Dan's coal black hair was damp, his jaw freshly shaven.
Two bloody nicks angled off from the deep scar cutting his
cheek. Hannah found herself following the white, healed
scar that ran down his cheek, jaw and throat. She shivered
unexpectedly, wanting to place the flat of her hand on Dan's
dark skin and smooth away the deep scar.

Hannah moved around Dan's tall body to stand facing
him. Shielded by her mirrored lenses, she examined each

rugged line of his face. Her stomach contracted painfully as she caught the silver at his temples and the bead of water clinging to the dark hair at the base of his throat.

He smelled of mountain winds and pine and sunlight.

"That's Fallcreek's old truck," Dan noted flatly, watching her carefully.

"The livestock," Hannah insisted while part of her went searching for Ethan's scents and couldn't find them. She'd been married, lived, worked and played with her husband for years, yet in a day, Dan had thrown Ethan into the shadows....

"I want to see your eyes when you look at me, Smokey." Dan lifted the large sunglasses from her and tucked them in his pocket.

"Dan..."

"Quite the sight—this scar of mine—isn't it?" he asked tightly as his head went back, his arrogance challenging her. "I've got a few calls to make before we load Macedonia."

"Macedonia? Uncle Earl's Appaloosa yearling?"

"He needed the vet and tending, and I brought him here," Dan said in a rough challenge, daring her to fight him. "He needs a home, the same as you.... If you don't want him, I do."

"You'd love that, wouldn't you? Ferguson stock—" she began.

"Leave it alone, Smokey. I'm the only one Macedonia will let near him since Earl died," he stated curtly before the telephone rang and he walked into the house.

Following the rigid straight line of his back, Hannah rubbed her gloved hand against her thigh. The stinging pain from the tumbleweeds didn't diminish the urge to smooth Dan's scar.

Dan opened the door and stood aside, waiting for her to enter. The interior of his home was dark and starkly barren, hallways angling off from a main living room. A huge rock fireplace, blackened by time and fitted with a practical black insert stove dominated the large room. Thick, hand-hewn beams, stark against the white plaster and scarred with time, shot across the ceiling. A handwoven cotton blanket lay tossed on the back of a large easy chair, the upholstery well used and the cushions sagging. Books lined one wall and Dan sat on the edge of a paper-cluttered desk, an antique solid-wood door placed over two filing cabinets. He clicked off the computer while he watched her and talked on the telephone.

The scent of coffee and wood smoke blended in the house and she glimpsed a neat kitchen. Windows lined one wall, spreading light on a small metal table covered with papers. A large, old enamel-and-chrome cooking stove with six burners and numerous doors lorded over the room. It cried out for the clutter of cooking, perhaps wooden utensils standing in a small crock.

The rooms were too neat, visually cold, serving the base need to shelter a man who worked outside in his waking hours.

She leaned against the rough planks covering a wall, trying to forget the last time she'd been in his house. "Make sure you stack those bales for her in the barn and range cubes, too. By the way, thanks for moving that Ferguson stock yesterday afternoon," Dan finished quietly, replacing the telephone to the cradle. He looked at her across the wide space of the room, waiting. "Do you want something to eat? There's chili in the slow-cooker."

Without waiting for an answer, his eyes went skimming down her, lighting suddenly as he looked at her rigid face. "Ponytail. Eyes that could set a man on fire, sweater and tight, long-legged jeans. Sassy, kissable mouth that promises everything.... You haven't changed a bit." His voice reminded her of a lover's hand in the dark of the night, stroking, caressing, heating, probing.

She shivered inside the hot-pink windbreaker, fighting her reaction to him. "Let's keep this on a business level. What's this about Macedonia?"

"He's been waiting for you." Dan stood, sliding his hands into his jeans' front pockets, thumbs out. A shaft of sun cut through the windows, laying a golden strip on the hardwood boards between them. Dan's scarred boot took a step into the sunlight. He crossed that golden strip, walking through the shadows to her. "You're pale and thin and look like you're riding on empty. Do you want to tell me about it?"

"Let's load the horse, Dan," she managed, fighting the urge to move into his arms.

"Sure," he whispered huskily. Bending slowly, giving her time to move away, Dan lowered his mouth to hers.

Poised amid shadows, sunlight and flashing, defiant anger, Hannah could not move.

Trapped by her senses, needing this one soft moment curling around her to ease the aching pain, Hannah waited.

Dan's kiss soothed, brushing, wooing, caressing the shape of her lips. Rubbing his parted mouth gently across hers, he breathed quietly, the warmth of his face and body spreading along hers. When his mouth lifted, Hannah fought to keep hers from following. "Take it easy, Hannah. We'll work it out together," he whispered softly, his breath caressing her cheek. "Welcome home."

He hadn't touched her, his hands safely in his pockets.

In another moment, Dan was gone. The door stood open and the sunlight shot through it. Dan's boots sounded on the porch's wooden planks.

Raising her trembling fingers to her lips, Hannah leaned against the wall for support. In that half minute, Dan had wrapped her in a tenderness she hadn't experienced in years. Taking a deep breath and fighting the dry ache behind her lids, Hannah slowly followed him.

Separated from Dan by a board fence, Macedonia ate grain from a feed trough. The Appaloosa stallion's mottled chestnut-and-white coat glistened, his mature lines still powerful. He looked up and whinnied as she approached.

"He was a yearling, prancing in the fields...Uncle Earl's—my father's delight," she corrected as emotions tightened her throat.

Dan's hand rested on her shoulder, easing up to gently rub the tight cords at the back of her neck. "Earl loved you. The horse was to be yours," he said softly.

She shivered, feeling the years rip through her, slicing through her with the pain of a knife. "I should have been here," she whispered unevenly.

Dan's fingers stopped their movement before he drew her against his side. "We all made mistakes along the way, Hannah," he murmured so softly that the soft breeze carried the sound out into the field.

She rubbed Macedonia's forehead slowly. "Did we? Or did I?" she asked, turning to look up at him. She didn't want his kindness—she wanted everything between them flung into the clean Wyoming sunshine. Everything with Ethan had been smooth, while her relationship with Dan had seared and soared with passionate anger—or when she was younger, sublime happiness. While Ethan soothed and encouraged, Dan caused an unforgettable excitement to pump through her. She thought of dark male textures blending with her own. Images of steam and passion and fire beckoned her. His incredibly tender kiss lingered on her lips, her breast suddenly heavy with the brand of his open palm.

I need you....

She needed to kiss his scar....

Nothing would be easy and halfway with Dan.... The sudden thought shot through her like fire and she raised her chin, squaring off with him. "Say it, Dan. Say how I should have come back and faced them all. I'm waiting. Take your best shot. You wrote those letters for Earl ... for my father, and you probably read mine in return, right?"

"Probably."

Her heart stopped beating at the pain in his eyes. His fingers brushed the ends of her ponytail, lingered in the sunlit strands, then slid away. He smiled slightly, turning up the collar of her windbreaker. "Ease up, Smokey. Guilt is a heavy burden."

Macedonia whinnied and Dan's black eyes shot down at her, setting off a hot wave of emotion she didn't understand. He caught her hand as she was about to thrust him away. "By the way, let's keep everything between you and me nice and clean. Mike's still wearing wounds from his divorce.... He doesn't stand a chance against you."

Ripples of stark anger went surging through her. "You've got nothing to say about it—"

Dan's smile was sensually knowing and wicked. His finger lifted to prowl across her lips before she could move away. "He's a nice guy. Leave him alone. When you think you're ready for that fandango, let me know."

His reference to a hot triple-time Spanish dance in which men and women teased each other with ever-increasing passion set her off. Her hand went slashing up to his face only to be caught in his. The collision burned her tender palm and she grimaced with pain.

In the next instant, he'd ripped her glove away and held her swollen, scratched palm up for his inspection. "What happened?" he demanded when she tore her hand away.

She lifted her hand for her glove and Dan slapped it into her palm, just hard enough to see her grimace. "Briars or tumbleweeds," he stated, watching her closely. "You think you can make it a year with hands as soft as a baby's bottom and perfume that can send a buffalo bull into heat, let alone set fire to every man within smelling distance?" he challenged darkly, striding to Jessie and starting the motor.

Dan slid the rear end of the pickup neatly into place next to the loading ramp. After Macedonia was loaded, Dan strode to her, scooped her up and slid her into the driver's seat, slamming the door. "Macedonia will back out by himself, once you're next to the ranch's loading ramp. He likes oats. The next time you raise your hand to me, be prepared to feel mine on your cute little backside."

"How arrogant!" she exploded, gripping the steering wheel and ignoring the burning pain of her palms. "I'm not a teenager looking up to you any longer. You've got about as much appeal to me as a belly-up rattler."

"Damn right, things have changed. You come after me this time, Smokey, and I'll tie you to the bed," he returned easily, his eyes challenging her on a level that frightened her.

She stared at him, trembling with anger. She wanted to tear out of the cab and launch herself at him, despite his size and strength. "Amazing how your mentality takes everything to the base level. Of course, your brain couldn't handle a civilized business relationship."

"First things first. The way I see our relationship has little to do with business."

After a moment in which she tried to think of a lashing reply, he said quietly, "When you want out of the will, let me know."

He slapped the side of Jessie's door and stood back. "Drive this thing slow. Old Macedonia isn't used to a fire woman."

"No wonder you haven't married, Dan," she said, sliding Jessie into first gear.

That evening Dan broke crackers into his chili, lifted the spoon to his mouth, then replaced it to the bowl. He stared at the flames dancing in the fireplace insert and tossed the movie script he'd been studying to the floor with his notes on the project. He slipped his glasses off and placed them on a side table.

He didn't want Hannah to know about the glasses. The glasses were a symbol of passing time that his pride did not want to recognize. A man's pride before a woman was sometimes all he had. He'd have his hands full, once she knew how desperate he was for her.

His side hurt like hell, the aftereffect of trying to work Hannah out of his system by cleaning the horses' stalls. Or was it riding Durango across the frozen fields until they both sweat?

Dan rubbed his palm against his jaw, remembering Hannah's flushed skin, her moist, parted lips. The sight of her torn hand had sent him over the edge, causing him to lose his temper. It was either pack her up within minutes or...

He'd seen a coyote chew off the paw caught in a trap, tearing off part of himself to survive. Now Dan felt the same way, tearing himself away from Hannah.

He rubbed the vein throbbing in his forehead and recognized the sharp edge of desire riding him. To tangle with her was bittersweet and he ached to hold her against him. In his excitement to see her this morning, he'd cut himself shaving. A shower and a change of clothing before noon wasn't his style, either. When everything else was stripped away, he had to admit that Hannah had gotten under his skin in double-time. Leaning his head back against the chair, Dan closed his eyes.

Hannah's lips were like rose petals sliding on silk, flowing warm and soft under his mouth. He'd wanted to comfort her, to wrap her in his arms and rock away her pain.

But it wouldn't stop there and he knew it. When he'd picked her up, his body told him to carry her into the house and make love to her, binding her to him. But he wanted her to see him coming. Wanted her free of the painful past.

Wanted her... Wanted her...

Dan looked out into the night. If ever there was a place he wanted to be, it was nestled in Hannah's arms. He'd spent years sitting in the same place, looking out at the same endless night. Then she'd come back, filling up the empty places in his life.

God help him if she ever found out he loved her.

Somehow he'd never pictured himself like a lovesick coyote baying at the moon. Or a randy cowboy, wearing his heart on his sleeve and watching soap operas while he dreamed of a love gone wrong. But there he was, staring at the big silvery hunter's moon and needing the low, husky sound of Hannah's voice.... She probably had an ex-husband mooning over her, a man who had heard the sounds she made while making love.

Was it the hot, spicy chili that caused Dan's stomach to burn? Or was it the thought of another man holding Hannah against him, in a tangle of sheets and long legs?

Still sitting in the same position a half hour later, he reached over and punched out her telephone number, listening for the sound of her voice, needing it to last throughout the lonesome night.

Hannah's sleepy, husky voice answered. "Mmm?"

"Watch those hands for infection," he said, smiling, knowing that those smoky gray eyes had just flung open.

Dan closed his eyes and imagined the sheets falling away from Hannah's breasts....

"Watch your backside, Blaylock. I'm going to kick it into the next county."

His grin widened; passion ran through him, heating him. "Sweet dreams, Hannah Louise."

Rising stiffly, Dan walked into the kitchen. In the shadows, the old stove gleamed and he ran his hand across the enamel, treasuring the dream that one day it would be lined with cooking pots and surrounded by his wife and children.

Empty years spread between his dream of marrying Hannah and the reality of her return. He lifted a dish towel from the oven handle and ran it slowly across the polished chrome. Dragging the stove from a nest of barn cobwebs, Dan had installed it in his home. Originally his mother's, nourishing Blaylock children until it was replaced by a newer, smaller model, the stove was designed to cook family meals or feed a large party. An oven and two broiler racks were beneath the burners. The left side was lined with an oven and warming oven and a wide shelf lay above the six burners. The massive forty-year-old stove represented the unused portion of his life.

At twenty-five, Dan had visualized Hannah standing at that stove, her body sheltering their unborn child. He'd dreamed of heating early morning milk bottles on that stove while Hannah slept in their bed, waiting for him to return.

He traced the scar on his face. Whatever Hannah had shared with Jordan, it wasn't a child.

He threw the towel aside, trying to force the need for Hannah away into the cold night.

Padding into the empty living room, he retrieved the movie script and his notes. The computer screen had been his friend throughout the nights, plugging holes in a scriptwriter's version of the West. Dan had worked with the lead actress, teaching her how to ride a horse. This time the director wanted Melissa Raven to learn about calf roping, using a double only if necessary.

Squiring Melissa to Hollywood premieres, in lieu of her traveling husband, had suited Dan perfectly in the past. Petite, blond and eager to further her career, Melissa treated Dan as a brother. She often brought her two-year-old son to his ranch during her visits.

Unlike Hannah, Melissa could be coached and pampered into following Dan's orders.

Hannah. Dan reached for his glasses, determined not to take another cold morning shower to ease his aroused body after a sleepless night. Hannah Louise and he had unfinished business and this time, he intended to wipe out the thought of any other man.

He stared at the computer screen, seeing Hannah as a child running to him, grinning about winning a prize at the county fair. Then, as a girl, just getting her first taste of flirtation. As a woman, she could drive him over the last bit of his sanity if he let her. He had the edge on her now, and he wasn't leaving this showdown with the blues.

Four

—

Hannah spent the next three days working in the November sunshine and fighting off dreams of Dan. Inch by inch, she cleaned the living room and cleared away enough of the kitchen clutter to be able to use the old gas stove and sink.

Straining, fighting her guilt and doubts, she worked until she couldn't think. Dan's image, stark and jarring, waited for her to rest. Slashing through her quiet moments, his tenderness reached out to her. *I need you.*

Lovemaking with Ethan, a gentle wisp of a memory, slithered out into the night without the slightest rousing of her senses. Yet Dan's infuriating, arrogant stance, his black eyes stripping away the thermal cloth covering her, his wide palm on her breast caused her breath to stop.

The tenderness of his kiss had warmed her palm, lingering on the soft flesh and promising a reverence and commitment she'd never experienced.

Skidding on thin emotional ice, she scrubbed the old tub harder. Her first recovery, the giant claw-footed tub dominating Earl's bathroom was pure luxury, even if she had to heat and carry water to fill it. When the plumber installed the new water heater, she'd purchase a circular shower curtain.

Scrubbed from ceiling to floor, the tiny room was lined with small well-varnished boards. Hannah had picked dry wildflowers for a bouquet, placing them in an old blue fruit jar on the wooden shelves. Another glass jar with a clamp-style lid contained moisturizing bath-oil beads. A basket she'd purchased for pennies at a yard sale hung on the wall, stuffed with new rolled mauve washcloths that matched the two thick bath towels drying on a white porcelain rod. The tank of the commode was the perfect place for a scarred wooden carpenter's tool case filled with soaps and toiletries. A nubby cotton throw rug covered the stripped-and-waxed tile floor and the louvered shutters on the bathroom's tiny window completed the country air.

The beauty of the small, restored room buoyed up Hannah's spirits each time she entered it. Steeped in the light of the copper oil lamp and the scents of the flowers and bath, the room offered Hannah the first peace she'd had since she'd arrived.

The frosty mornings were perfect and cleansing, filling her with a calm she hadn't felt in years. Working until nine in the morning, she used the next two hours to calculate feed and hay costs and make business calls. The remainder of the days were spent in the clear warm sunshine, sorting tools and nailing down shingles.

She enjoyed looking at the stock, sensing her father's serene pleasure as the buffalo grazed quietly in a sheltered valley or Hereford calves playfully butted each other.

Like glittering golden coins constantly flipped by fortune's hand, her thoughts moved through the past and into the future. Her father. Earl. Camelot, the ranch of his dreams. Macedonia, the yearling, now the stallion almost past his prime.

Hovering over everything was the mystery of how her parents' and Earl's bills had been paid. What kept the Ferguson land title free from an auctioneer's call for bidders? The answer led back to Dan. Though the land was largely underdeveloped and hilly, studded with forests, the Camelot would enlarge his smaller spread by acres.

All Dan needed to do was wait for her failure.

He wasn't going to get the pleasure.

Prying off the boards nailed across the windows suited Hannah's mood. Straining against the crowbar, tearing the nails from the wood siding, she pictured prying Dan's overlord tentacles from her land.

Hannah leaned her weight into the crowbar and dismissed borrowing against her trust. She wanted to wrest the ranch from Dan's clutches without any help from money earned with Ethan or the years she'd spent away. The rusty nails gave way just as she said, "I can...do it...."

Holding the board and the crowbar in her gloved hands, she turned to Macedonia, who had been watching her carefully from the barn lot. "Thank you. Your confidence in me means everything."

Big Al bellowed loudly from a rolled knoll and Hannah waved back. "Thank you, guy."

A new red farm pickup turned off the main highway, approaching the house. When it parked in front of the house, Hannah recognized the driver. She dropped the board at her feet and placed the crowbar over it. Straightening, she stripped her gloves off and tucked them in her jeans pocket. According to Mort Raznick, Bernadette had happily married a Blaylock brother, James. In short, they had added three children to the community census.

After sixteen years, Bernadette had that happy, broody look, though her smile was now forced. "Hi, Hannah. I was just passing by...oh, the heck with that...." She lifted a casserole dish and a brown-paper sack from the pickup. "Are you ready for lunch?"

"Are you buying?" Hannah tossed back, smiling.

"Lasagna, salad and chocolate cake." Bernadette's brown eyes slid down Hannah's sweatshirt and long legs encased in jeans. "Wow! No wonder James says Dan is in for woman trouble."

Ignoring the years and the last showdown with Dan, and remembering the good teen years, Hannah grinned. "Neat-o to the lunch—yuck-o to Dan. Let's go inside."

After the marvelous meal, Bernadette hadn't lost her forced smile, though she carried on a steady dialogue about her husband and children. With the nervous air of a person who expected to be turned down, she said, "Are you going to show me the mansion or what? Have broom, will work.... You've got me until the school bus drops Jessie on us. The other two are staying for cheerleading practice.... Remember when we were high school cheerleaders?"

Hannah suddenly realized how badly she needed the special friendship she and Bernadette had shared as teenagers. "I am so happy for you, Bernie. And I'm snatching up your offer right this minute.... The kitchen dirt might be bigger than the both of us. From the looks of it, it hasn't been cleaned in years."

Bernadette's eyes twinkled. "Should we let Gertrude, your new barn cat, loose first? She's in a box in the pickup, just waiting to start mousing."

Three hours later the kitchen gleamed and two tired friends leaned against the counter to study their work. Bernadette pointed to an old ladder propped against the wall. "That thing is worthless. Let's carry it out."

Hannah wriggled her sock-covered toes against Gertrude's belly until she purred outrageously. "Nope, but you can help me lift it to those ceiling hooks."

When Bernadette lifted her eyebrows, Hannah explained. "I need an indoor clothes dryer now—and a washer—but I'm hoping to hang and dry herbs and flowers from it later. Maybe a few hanging plants to catch the light from the windows."

"How marvelous! You make me just want to go home and start cleaning James's toolshed." Bernadette's eyes softened. "How I love that man, Hannah. I just wish..."

Bernadette leaned closer, her expression urgent. "Oh, Hannah. None of these sixteen years would have happened if I hadn't been so silly, so jealous of you. I just wanted to show Dan and everyone around here that I was as good as you. You can't know how I've hated myself for that night.... For trying to get Dan's eyes to light up the way they did when he looked at you. It was a dumb kid thing to do. I stripped and slipped into his shower, thinking that—then you were there and all hell broke loose. Even back then, I could see that Dan never wanted anyone but you. But don't get the idea that James Blaylock is second-best with me.... I love that man down to his ornery Apache-Spanish bones."

Hannah studied Bernadette's anxious expression and spoke carefully. They were two women now, not teenagers discussing an infatuation while styling their hair and painting their fingernails. Bernadette had been her friend years ago and she wanted friendship to ripen. "You've got nothing to do with what's between Dan and myself, Bernie. I want you for my friend."

"Oh, Hannah..." Bernadette hugged her. "That's just what James said. I've been so worried...."

"There's just one thing I want you and the Blaylocks to know, Bernie," Hannah added carefully after returning the hug. "Daniel Blaylock and I are set for a showdown. It's no wonder no woman would ever have him. My boot marks are going to be all over his backside, but good."

"Uh-huh...that's just what James told Dan. That's exactly why Dan is riding Sweet Pea Yokum—Logan's bucking bull—in Saturday's local rodeo.... Some macho stuff that only God understands, when everyone in two counties knows that Dan is really a softie.... There's a dance later, in case you're interested."

Saturday morning, dressed in her jeans and a sweater, Hannah leaned back from the papers spread on Doug Fallcreek's large desk at the bank. When she had asked for a loan, Doug had tactfully explained the Ferguson family's long-standing economic problems. Earl had assumed her parents' debts, ultimately spiraling into a tight-money situation. "Do you mean that Dan has been supporting the Camelot and my uncle for years? That he'd acquired enough money from the rodeo circuit and advising Western moviemakers to—"

Hannah thought of the battered Flying H pickup and the tidy one-man ranch, her frown deepening.

"I'm going to step out from behind this desk, and level with you," Doug said quietly. "Dan's finances started with a healthy grubstake. I've advised him to let go of the Ferguson land or it would take him down, the same as it had Earl and your parents." Doug's voice softened. "I'm sorry, but your uncle was a dreamer, Hannah. Not a businessman. Dan is tough and he's making slow financial progress. But nothing like he would have without the Camelot under his wing. He's paid off the mortgage and has been managing both spreads at the same time."

"Because he stands to gain Ferguson land. He could sell it off easily and still come out ahead," she stated hotly.

Doug tapped his pencil on the Ferguson accounts. "Hannah, you look like you're riding on the edge. Putting together your life and working on the ranch until you drop at the same time can't be easy. There's a perspective in Dan's helping with the ranch that you might be overlooking.... Have you ever thought that—"

He glanced at her flushed face, took a deep breath and said quietly, "At this point, with Dan holding the reins, I'm afraid any mortgage with your signature would be difficult to explain to our investors. If you want to try again after the year, I'll be happy to talk business."

At one o'clock that afternoon, Hannah entered the rodeo grounds and began working her way to the board bleachers. She smiled and talked with old friends and met new ones. The Blaylock males courteously dipped their Western hats to her and tended their ladies gallantly.

Fiftyish and pretty, Sally Demornay touched her hand. "Bernie says you're a decorator and that you could help me solve a tiny problem in the house. The thing is, with all four kids in college, we're avoiding extra expenses. I was just wondering—oh, shoot...I might as well come right out with it. Now that the kids are gone, things are getting...frisky at our house, if you know what I mean."

In another moment she added briskly, "Bernie says you need some things, and well...I've always wanted a bedroom—a sexy boudoir to seduce Mr. Jimmy Demornay right out of his boots. What do you say to a trade?''

''I'd say you're on,'' Hannah returned with a grin that died when the rodeo parade into the arena began. Seated on the sun-warmed bleachers next to Bernadette, Hannah straightened, focusing on Dan's broad back.

Bearing flags and riding prancing, groomed horses, the riders circled the arena, each carrying a small bouquet of flowers. The women riders tossed the bouquets to husbands and children, the men and boys to sweethearts, wives and children.

Dan reined Durango to a stop directly in front of Hannah. The show saddle decorated with silver disks glittered in the sun. Then suddenly, his spray of baby's breath and lush dark red roses arced high into the air, sailing straight toward Hannah through the blue sky.

When she caught them, Dan's head went back, the black hat shielding a hot, daring look that she met evenly. He tugged down the brim of his hat, a blend of challenge and courtesy.

''Trouble,'' Bernadette murmured quietly beside Hannah.

''Dan Blaylock just bought it,'' Hannah returned evenly as she stood. Taking her time, she ripped the petals from the roses. Allowing them to catch the slight breeze and drift away, she tossed the bouquet back to him and blew a kiss from her fingertips.

''Oh-oh,'' Sally whispered when Dan swept off his hat and swept it in front of him in a mock bow.

The calf-roping and barrel-racing events preceeded the bull riding. Then Sweet Pea Yokum, two tons of bucking bull, crashed against the wooden chute trying to dislodge Dan, who was steadily easing down into riding position.

Logan came to sit beside her, and ten-year-old Patty quickly perched on his lap. Looking like all the Blaylocks, tall and rawly male, with shining black hair, Logan's expression was hard. ''My little brother could get himself stomped good out there,'' he said quietly, watching Dan adjust his hand through the bull rope encircling Sweet Pea's barrel belly.

The flip return dried on Hannah's tongue. "Yes, he could," she agreed softly.

The gate opened. Like a single beast charging from hell, man and animal tore across the frozen earth in powerful bucking circles. When the eight-second bell sounded, Hannah found her heart had begun to beat again.

In the course of those long eight seconds, she'd just discovered that no one had ever meant as much to her as Daniel Blaylock.

If he'd been hurt, she'd have run to him.

If he'd died beneath the horns and hooves of Sweet Pea, part of her—

Hannah bit her lip just as Logan said quietly, "Hannah, you're hurting my hand."

She looked down at her long, pale fingers gripping Logan's large, dark hand. She forced her hand away, shocked when he spread his fingers slowly; the impression of his wedding band sank into the neighboring flesh. She licked her lip and found the salty taste of blood. When she looked up, trapped by her emotions, Logan's dark eyes met hers. "He's been waiting for you."

"Oh, no..." she whispered brokenly. Years, separation and her marriage hadn't changed her need for Dan one bit. The shattering thought went zinging around her as Dan turned suddenly and stared at her across the distance of the arena.

The wild ride had swept his hat away, revealing a rolled red kerchief that served as a sweatband. He stood, boots locked to the hard-packed arena floor, broad shoulders back, dusty and sweaty from his faded red shirt to his weathered chaps. His eyes narrowed and his jaw hardened beneath the dust covering his dark, gleaming skin. Nothing soft, nor kind wooed her tenderly.

He'd waited and now he was set on taking.

The roar of the crowd faded as she placed her hand over her throat, protecting the fast-beating pulse there.

Tanned and rough, Dan's desire for her shimmered in the golden November sunlight.

Over her skin, her fingertips trembled. *Because she wanted him just as desperately.* Lodged firmly in her past, Dan loomed in her future. Unshakable. Able to send her emotions flying into the blue sky like a red balloon riding a high wind.

Then he turned away. Hannah rubbed her hands against her thighs, drying her palms. To keep her hands from shaking, she gripped the wooden bleacher just as the announcer began to call out the prizewinners.

Hannah firmed her lips. She would not run. Not this time. She could fight whatever Daniel Josiah Blaylock threw at her.

When her fingers stopped trembling, she stood to leave the bleachers. Somehow she smiled and talked, moving with the crowd toward the exit.

She turned and Dan stood over her.

She didn't want him to see. To examine, with his hunter's quick eyes, her emotions before she knew them herself. When she tried to brush past him, Dan's hand on her upper arm held her back.

Her head went back, fury building in her. "So you can still ride," she shot at him. "Congratulations on the prize money."

"You called out my name just before the bell," he murmured, his thumb caressing the side of her breast covered by her flannel-lined denim jacket. "As though you cared."

Hannah inhaled sharply, remembering suddenly the cry of fear sliding across her lips. The way her heart had sailed out of her to him. "Try someone else, Dan," she said between her teeth.

Why did part of her want to wrap her arms around him, holding him fiercely tight? Oh, God, how she had prayed for his safety in those dangerous eight seconds.

"The hell it was some other woman who called out my name," he clipped out before lowering his tone. "No one has a voice like yours. Like the hot July wind sweeping through the pines...or a scent like an exotic hothouse flower."

The images his low voice portrayed seared her, raking at her tangled emotions. "Let me go. No one told you to mix in Ferguson land. To pay off Earl's mortgage. To sacrifice your own—"

"Honey, take it easy." Dan's mouth lowered to brush hers lightly and she tried to remember what she was saying as her eyes slowly closed.

So soft, warm, rubbing, caressing, cherishing... The kiss lasted just a millisecond, but when his lips lifted, she ached for more.

Shaken by her emotions, wanting to return the kiss, wanting to... Hannah jerked her arm free. Her voice was husky, vibrating unevenly in an uncertain tone. "You won't get paid back that way."

"Money doesn't have a thing to do with this, and from the looks of those shadows under your eyes, you know it," Dan whispered just as unevenly, his fingers sliding around her narrow wrist. "Time to face reality—"

Much too aware of his thumb stroking the sensitive inner skin of her wrist, Hannah's head went back at the open challenge. Her pulse throbbed rapidly beneath his warm touch before it slid away, baring her skin to the autumn chill. "You're saying I can't deal with you?"

Dan tilted his head to one side, his arms folded across his chest in that cocksure arrogance that made her want to fling herself at him. "Tell you what," he said slowly, watching her. "Jasmine's Fandango is tonight. You show me just how good you are at dealing with me."

He lifted a strand of her hair, ran his thumb across the fiery tips and added softly, "Unless you can't take the heat. I can understand if you want to hole up when everyone else is having a good time."

"Dan, you don't know what you're asking for—" she warned, fighting the way his eyes had locked with hers.

"Don't I?" he asked softly, stepping near.

The sensual maelstrom had sucked her softly under, her body aware of his heat. "Not in this lifetime, Dan," she whispered, her throat suddenly dry.

* * *

The barn-dance social used a Spanish-Western theme, blending flamenco guitar with square dances and callers. After a potluck dinner featuring deer and fish, the tables were cleared away for dancing.

Composed of neighbors, the band set a fast pace. In a myriad of Western and Spanish dress, the dancers collided and swirled through polkas, square dancing, waltzing and an occasional jitterbug. Stately elderly couples mixed with teens waiting for a cassette of rock during the band's break. Skirting the dance floor, children danced together and with their grandparents. Teens eyed each other shyly and waited for the "right" song. Punch, apple cider, cake and cookies were served, and a nursery was provided for sleepy children.

Blaylocks of all ages dominated the closely knit community "do," clearly interested in Hannah's reaction to Dan. She'd set out to let the countryside know that whatever Dan threw her way, she could walk away unscathed. Dressed in a Spanish peasant costume borrowed from Bernadette, Hannah tied a vivid fringed shawl around the waist and one hip of her full gathered skirt. She'd deliberately lowered the elastic of the white eyelet bodice to frame her shoulders and piled her hair loosely on top of her head with large, flashy combs. Adding just a touch of cosmetics to define her wide-set eyes and strong cheekbones, Hannah met Dan's gaze evenly.

Wearing jeans and a long-sleeved red shirt rolled back at the forearms, Dan was easily spotted in the churning, happy crowd. His dark skin and strong features met her at every turn. They passed in a fast square dance, his arms bringing her tightly, possessively against his taut body. His thighs moved sensuously against her and his hand went sliding down her hips before she swung away. The fiery look she shot his way collided with a scathing frown that deepened when the blouse slipped low on her shoulder.

The next time they passed, Dan pulled her close against him and bent to whisper harshly in her ear. "That's quite some getup, Smokey. Enough to set fire to every man here."

She pushed at his shoulder, the hard muscle resisting her palm as he held her closer, keeping the beat of the music. She wanted him at her feet, as hurt as she had been years ago. Nothing could stop her from slashing at him. "Including yourself?"

"I figure that anything you get is coming to you," he said between his teeth, smoothing the indented line of her waist and hip with his long fingers.

"Likewise," she returned, allowing her body to flow into his.

His harsh breath brushed her hot cheek. "Don't square off with me—unless you want to deal with the consequences."

"Why don't you leave my thinking to me?"

His smile wasn't nice, the scar zigzagging down his dark cheek as he studied the wisps of hair escaping the combs and the flush riding her face. "Ask me nice and I'll help you through the year. Or I can buy the land flat-out right now. Fight me and I'll win."

As she walked away, her body rigid with anger, Hannah thought she heard him chuckle.

The next dance was a fandango, the Spanish music rippling through the room with fire-hot intensity. A few dancers tried the music while the rest waited for another dance. But the announcer, used to priming his balking neighbors into action, took the microphone. "Come on folks... Is that the best Jasmine can do? Let's put some life into it. Ladies' choice... Ladies, grab that gent."

Because the music suited her mood, stoking her temper and daring her to grind Dan into the dance floor, Hannah straightened her shoulders and headed straight across the dance floor toward Dan. He'd ordered her not to square off with him, the challenge ringing in her ears as their eyes locked.

Cradling sleeping three-year-old Mattie Blaylock on his hip and sipping a cup of hot mulled cider, Dan met her eyes as she closed the distance. He rocked slowly side to side, nuzzling the child's black hair with a kiss while he tracked Hannah across the room.

She hesitated in mid-stride, memories flying at her like darting hungry birds. She'd wanted his children, dreamed about having them once so long ago... ached to create life with him. Forcing the memory away, Hannah continued making her way toward him. Nothing could keep her from meeting him, challenging him tonight.

Dan's eyes darkened, his mouth firming. Taking his time, he placed the cup on a side table and eased Mattie to her mother's arms. Holding Hannah's eyes, Dan bent to kiss the girl's cheek, then straightened slowly. In a timeless Western stance, fingers slid into his front pockets and thumbs hooked into his belt, Dan watched her come toward him. Every rugged plane of his face locked into a challenge of wills.

Emily Blaylock tossed her a pair of castanets with an *"Olé."*

Nothing could have stopped Hannah, except an earthquake opening the ground between Dan and herself. She'd waited aeons to best him and now she would....

As a teenager she'd seen Dan dance the fandango, and now the memory clawed at her. She took a deep breath, noting the slow trail of Dan's eyes down her bodice, then back up to her face. Whatever happened, Daniel Blaylock wasn't remembering the fandango with any other woman after tonight.

She intended to dance him into the hardwood boards and step over his body to continue her life.

The guitar music rippled up and down, catching on her spine when she stopped just inches from Dan. "Can you handle this, Blaylock?" she asked, high on the excitement dancing between them.

Whatever emotion Dan stirred within her, she wanted that edge tonight. Wanted to feel her pulses throbbing, the heat of stepping out of the shadows, wanted nothing but the hard challenge of the music and the man's sensuality beating against her. The music offered a purge of tangled emotions, and she sensed that only Dan could withstand the wild tempo and heat.

Dan nodded, a strand of black hair crossing his forehead. She experimented, clicking the wooden castanets between fingers and palm. "Cute," he said, noting the heavy pulse in her throat that lifted the tiny gold locket. His dark gaze lowered to her breasts, boldly traced the hardening nubs beneath the light cotton cloth, then rose to her face. "So you want to play...."

When they stepped onto the floor, the years fell away from Hannah as she remembered the intricate steps. Straightening, her body arched, tautly erect, her heels beating against the boards, Hannah lifted her arms above her head and turned, castanets clicking. Stepping close, then quickly away, they circled each other and the crowd slid into the shadows.

Heads high and bodies straight, they stared at each other. Dan's boots beat a steady tempo on the hardwood floor, his hands behind his back. Hannah's body arched toward him, her arms raised high to click the castanets.

Feinting, ever moving closer only to move apart, they danced the fandango. Stepping daringly close, his hands clasped behind his back, Dan allowed his body to brush hers, his eyes daring her to step away.

Meeting his challenge, Hannah raised her face to his, her feet matching his steps.

Riding on the edge, wrapped in nothing but the music and the heat, Hannah strained against the limits of time and memory.

Dan was hers now, their bodies and minds moving together....

Her hair came loose, the combs falling to the floor. Dan's black hair spiked with sweat, his eyes dark and fathomless beneath his lashes as the tempo increased. "You red-haired witch," he murmured, breathing hard. His rakish grin first stunned her, then sent her soaring.

She laughed then, let it bubble out of her as she shot him a daring sidelong glance and started moving around him. In traditional style, Dan was forced to keep his hands firmly locked behind him. Yet his eyes followed her, tangling the past and present together.

Stepping close and daring him to stop, Hannah grinned. "You're too old to keep up, Blaylock. You'll fold first."

"Uh-uh." Snaking a hand to her hip, he unknotted the shawl and whipped it around her waist. Holding the edges of the cloth behind him, Dan forced her body against his hard one.

Lowering her hands to behind her back and keeping the castanets clicking slowly, Hannah gave herself to the moment. The heat of his body steamed into hers, his thighs moving closely against her own. The music changed to a slower beat, his body moving tightly with hers; his scent enclosed her as they danced.

Without a pause, the music moved into a smooth waltz. Keeping the traditional Spanish dance position, Dan moved her around the floor, gliding her through the other couples.

Then they were outside moving through the shadows of the town hall's veranda. Scents of wood smoke and pine drifted on the light breeze as Dan closed a door behind him.

When the lock clicked Hannah blinked and found herself tangled in the shadows and Dan's strong arms.

The room was empty and cold, moonlight crossing into the room from the enormous windows.

Above her, Dan's face was harsh. Taking his time, he placed his palms along her cheeks, framing her face, fingers spearing through the tousled mass of her hair.

Her fingers trembled, curled into fists at her sides as his mouth slowly lowered. Fitting his lips carefully over hers, sealing her breath with his, Dan shivered. He nibbled at the contours of her mouth as if tasting her, delighting in the texture of her skin, her warmth. His thumbs moved near her jaw, caressing the underside, and down her throat. Moving her against a wall, he leaned into her body with a long sigh and deepened the light kiss.

She was holding him then, sliding her palms flat against the rippling planes of his back, taking his warmth into her.

Lifting and parting her lips for his, feeding on the tender, tantalizing brush of his, Hannah forced herself to breathe quietly.

His kisses moved across her lids, his uneven breath warm against her face. His large, rough hands slid to encircle her throat, tracing her collarbone lightly. Each touch explored, tantalized and heated before moving on, the texture of his face rough against hers. Easing closer, his heartbeat heavy against her chest, Dan looked down at her.

Slowly unbuttoning his shirt and dropping it to the floor, he placed her hands on his chest. Rubbing them against him, letting her take his heat and prowl the hard power sheathed beneath the hair-roughened surface, Dan watched her face.

She'd seen him angry and in pain and happy. But his expression now bound her like a magical web. The aching tenderness and desire stripped her defenses bare, leaving her with a need to answer.... "We can stop at any time, Smokey," he murmured rawly. "Just touch me...."

In that moment, she knew that no man had ever wanted her with the power and force of Dan Blaylock.

With a reverence that stunned her, Dan's hands trembled, sliding to her bare shoulders. Easing aside the elasticized neckline, his fingertips slid across her sensitive skin, steadily lowering the peasant blouse.

She wanted to move away.

Instead she leaned against him, taking his strength and his warmth. He shuddered, his large hands stroking the blouse down to her waist. Following his touch, his gaze slid to her lacy beige bra.

The vulnerable, haunting expression of his eyes reached down to her from the shadows. "You are so beautiful," he whispered, his fingertips stroking a path to the poignant tip of the lace and circling it. He drew her slowly against him, closing his lashes as though to absorb her into his hot skin, his arms moving to encircle her.

Beneath her lips, his skin tasted like salt and desire. His heart slammed against her palm, his body hard against hers. "Hold me," he ordered roughly, breathing hard. "Put your arms around me and hold on tight."

Arching, pitting her body against his, needing the storm and the peace Dan offered, Hannah slid her arms around his neck. Sliding through her fingers, his hair was sleek and warm as Dan eased her deeper into the shadowy corner.

Then his mouth touched her breast and she couldn't move, her breath trapped inside her. "Fight me, tell me to stop," he whispered roughly. His bare shoulders rippled beneath her fingers, the heat between their bodies driving away the cold.

Fighting the melting heat weakening her legs, aware of the heaviness of his thighs pressing into hers, Hannah wanted Daniel Blaylock more than air. The thought frightened her until she trembled.

His hands, warm and rough, moved gently to claim her. She'd made love with Ethan, but Dan's passion fired her own, erasing the past. She could taste him on her mouth, her body answering the bold thrust of his....

Was this how Iris had felt about Earl? Wanting to slip inside his skin? The hunger to take and give, to taste and feel everything at once? To become part of him?

To ride out the storms with him? To cradle his head on her breast and stroke away the aftermath of the fierce desire?

In a blink of time, she'd discovered the secret of her birth....

Hannah fought back the tears burning at her lids. "Dan...I..."

When a single tear trailed down her cheek and fell, Dan's body tensed. He stopped stroking her, his heart beating hard. Cradling her head with his hand, he bent to slowly kiss her lids. "Shh...Shh..."

Tucking her face in the shelter of his neck and shoulder, Dan encircled her with his arms and stood, rocking her quietly when the first sobs ripped through her.

Clinging to him, knowing he could withstand the emotions riding her, Hannah cried for the first time in sixteen years.

Five

Three days later, Else Murphy's red four-wheel-drive Blazer stood in front of Dan's ranch house. His oldest sister poured coffee into his mug, then sat across the table from him. As Jasmine's leading matriarch, Else served freshly baked bread and advice with equal care. Marked by the Blaylock's big, lean frame, Else wielded her matriarchal prod in a manner rivaling a top engineer; she considered Dan's bachelor status as the challenge of her career. "I'm going over to Hannah's later," she stated, watching him. "Taking her some of my jams and preserves, a few jars of pickles and so forth...just to make her feel welcome. Poor little thing. Here she is, not a family to come home to and you snarling at everyone around."

"So?" He ate Else's renowned German chocolate cake and sipped his coffee. This morning a dressy sweater set and slacks replaced Else's usual jeans and she wore their mother's pearl earrings. Dan glanced at them uneasily; when Else put on those earrings, she meant business.

"You two put on quite the show at the Fandango. Then Miss Hannah disappeared and you turned up acting like a wounded wolf. That sort of thing makes for gossip, Dan."

"So?" Dan sat back in his chair. When Else decided to speak her mind, there was little anyone could do. Twenty years older than Dan, she had worried about "the shape of his life" for years.

"You're getting old, Dan. Old and ornery. You'll end up like Jacob Sellars, a bachelor dying out in the hills alone. His dog wouldn't even stay with him at the end. Remember your German shepherd mix and that little terrier that ran off to homes with children?"

"Is there a moral to this story, Else?" Dan turned his blue granite mug around carefully, inspecting the spots. He respected Else, knowing that she thought carefully before interfering in his life. But his relationship with Hannah wasn't something that required Else's fine touch.

"Daniel Josiah Blaylock, I've been waiting for you to bring Miss Hannah over to our ranch. Of course, I imagine she's too busy with Mike, Mark Kincaid and B.J. Fairhair—"

"Why the hell should I care?" Dan shot at her, scowling. Since Hannah strolled back into Jasmine, the curious pointed-ear look of the community's single men had sharpened. But when Else decided to mix in Dan's affairs, she preferred to lay her chewed bones at his feet.

Else smiled serenely and placed another piece of cake on his plate. "Don't take that tone of voice with me, Dan. I've worried about you since you had diaper rash, but I'm getting a little tired of the job and would really like to give your reins to another unfortunate woman. You've let Miss Hannah slip through your fingers for years. Now she's back, the bachelors' blood is running hot, the countryside is stirred up, and you sit out here like a wolf baying at the moon."

Else touched her left earring, straightening it. "You get yourself over there. Slide off that high horse for a bit and show her how much you care.... You've loved that baby girl from the moment you held her in your arms, but you've got that Blaylock pride and stubborn streak."

Dan shot her a dark look. "Don't you have grandchildren who need tending? Or a sick person who needs chicken broth? Mind your own business, Else."

She smiled and patted his hand. "But I am, dear little brother. I took over the job from Mother.... Try a little understanding when you talk to Hannah. I figure she's probably the only chance I have for a sister-in-law from you. You evaded giving grandchildren to our dear departed parents, but you are not going to escape me. Just stop snarling, eat your cake and do what I say."

Dan stared at her, acknowledging her skill at backing him into a corner. "I'm not pining away for Hannah."

"Uh-huh," she agreed easily. "That's why you named this ranch after her—the Flying H for Hannah. When am I going to be holding your offspring on my lap? I have rights, you know, and seeing you happy is one of them. Whatever you're doing wrong with Hannah, you stop it. And don't forget to tip your hat when she's around, like Mama said. Blaylock men are noted for their courtly ways and you're not sullying their reputation. She's got her pride, the same way you do. Tend it with care."

The first week of December, Dan slid out of Durango's saddle to stand on the knoll overlooking the Ferguson ranch house. He turned up his collar against the bitter morning wind and propped his boot on a fallen pine log.

Sighting down on Hannah, he watched her put the strong three-year-old gelding through his paces on the frozen snow-covered field. Sired by Macedonia and James's buckskin mare, Apache pitted his will against the woman riding him. Suddenly straining against the reins, the gelding stretched out his legs to cover the field, flying by the cattle and the buffalo.

In a bulky sweatshirt and jeans, Hannah's leggy body fitted the old saddle perfectly. Her ponytail caught in the wind as she leaned forward, urging the gelding to run with all his power.

Dan's fingers tightened on Durango's reins and the horse whinnied softly. "She's tough...riding him down...taking everything he has...." Dan murmured quietly, aware that any moment Apache might step into a gopher or prairie-dog hole and Hannah's lovely neck could be broken.

He had plans for that silky length of neck, he decided darkly. Something hot and wild waited in Hannah. The night of the Fandango he'd stirred it to simmering. Brushed it with his hands and mouth and frightened her badly.

The sight of her face, pale and aching in the moonlight had stopped him immediately.

Her sobs echoed in his mind like the wind rustling in the leaves at his feet. For two sleepless weeks, he'd tried to tear the sounds from him and yet they returned.

Why had she cried? Did she want Jordan? The thought slammed into Dan as though for the first, not the hundredth time.

"Damn." Dan's mouth tightened when Apache lengthened his stride, headed for a high board fence separating the ranch from three hundred acres of untamed Ferguson spread. In a heartbeat, Hannah's body leaned low into the flying leap over the fence.

For an aeon, woman and beast were etched against the gray threatening clouds.

Dan's heart began to beat again when the gelding cleared the top board and landed safely in the two-inch powdery snow. Hooves flying, throwing frozen sod and snow high into the air, the horse and Hannah snaked through a shallow valley and crossed a tiny ice-covered creek.

Dan found himself in Durango's saddle, cutting through the heavy stand of pine trees toward Hannah. The flying beat of Durango's hooves matched the heavy sound of his heart.

The gelding fought his way up a steep embankment, starting a tiny slide. At the very crest, a chunk of earth gave way and the horse struggled for solid ground. Rocks and snow sailed out into the air, then plummeted to the stream below, cracking the ice.

Was it the sound of Durango's flying hooves or the sound of his heartbeat echoing in his ears? "Damn her," Dan cursed between his teeth as the horse found his footing and slowly circled the high ground, prancing proudly.

He slowed Durango, fighting hard to control his fear and his anger as the horse moved carefully down the embankment.

Apache took his own sweet time prancing back to the fence he had just cleared. Dan bent to swing open the rusty gate and Hannah grinned triumphantly back at him, ripping her earmuffs from her head.

"You look about fifteen years old," he said quietly, surprising himself as he tugged his hat in greeting.

She patted Apache's damp coat, rubbing him with her glove. Flushed with her victory and the cold wind, Hannah's voice was soft with pride. "He's gorgeous. Smooth as silk."

The next instant, she rounded on Dan. Sweeping back a strand of hair that had slipped free, Hannah walked Apache toward Dan. "What are you doing here? Checking up on me?"

Easing back in the saddle and walking Durango beside her, Dan admired the high, proud set of her head, the dull fire of her hair. Else's advice and his good intentions sailed into the cold wind. Seeing Hannah had set him on an edge he recognized easily, but could not alter, any more than he could change winter into summer. "No need to. The local boys are keeping tabs on you."

Big Al sauntered from the buffalo grazing in a sheltered valley and raised his nose to the wind. He began to bellow, digging up clods of snow with his hooves. Apache sidestepped quickly and Dan's hand shot out to control the reins. "Let go of my horse," Hannah ordered quietly, her gray eyes heating.

"One of you is going to end up with a broken neck." Dan continued to hold the bridle, walking Durango beside Apache. "After a ride like that, cool your horse down. And tell Mike to stay the hell away."

Hannah's eyes widened. "Mike?"

"Mike," Dan answered grimly, knowing that he handled his emotions and the situation wrong. "Our divorced and lonesome sheriff."

Hannah took a deep breath, her fingers gripping the saddle horn. "Dan, your fist may be clutching Ferguson land, but that doesn't give you the right—"

He leaned over to kiss her hard and fast, stopping the hot flow of words. "Maybe not," he said quietly as she stared at him. "But that does. Mark Kincaid is spouting off about working all night on your plumbing, and B.J. Fairhair is getting worked up to asking you to dinner. B.J.'s fiancée wasn't happy.... They just broke up."

Hannah frowned, glancing at the dark, low clouds as she rubbed the back of her glove across her mouth. "Mark did work all night on the plumbing and B.J. delivered several cords of wood...."

"Dave Johnson helped you move furniture from Bernadette's. Seems like you've got enough help." Dan noted the plastic covering the house windows and tried to forget the way her lips had clung to his for just an instant before the kiss ended.

The freezing wind sailed between them. Hannah stared at him for a moment, her eyes darkening. "Did you drop over to gossip, Dan? Or is there a purpose to your visit?"

"Winter is coming, Miss Hannah. If something goes wrong out here, you could freeze to death in your sleep," he returned slowly, suddenly wanting to hold her against him. To shelter her from whatever pain she carried. The echo of her cries swept along on the freezing wind as Dan walked Durango beside Apache.

Her head went higher, the wind whipping at her ponytail, and Dan's fingers ached to run through the silky strands....

"I wouldn't endanger Ferguson stock by freezing to death, Dan," she stated flatly. "Would you like to come in the house to check the stoves? I've got a wood heater and an electric stove. There's an electric wall heater in the bathroom and in the kitchen."

"I'd like a cup of coffee, if you're offering," he answered slowly, watching the throbbing vein in her throat. He ached to taste the sweet flesh over it, to feel her blood beat hot and fast beneath his lips. "After that, I'll fix that hole in the barn roof."

She turned to him, her face pale. "I don't need your help, Dan. Don't touch anything. I'll get to it. Playing the friendly helping-neighbor role doesn't suit you."

"Maybe not." Dan swung down from his horse and held Apache's reins as Hannah slid to the ground, glaring up at him. The bones of her face pushed against her taut skin, dark circles framing her gray eyes. She'd been pushing hard, fighting to wrest him from Ferguson land. "You're cold, Hannah," he said quietly, "Go on to the house. I'll rub down Apache."

"Dan..." she began to protest before he leaned down to kiss her mouth lightly. He wanted to hold her in his arms, protect her from the pain of the past.

"Move it," he ordered softly, watching the confusion in her expression. Whatever was there between them, lying in the past and waiting in the future, Hannah knew it existed.

When he entered the small kitchen, Hannah had stripped her layers of sweatshirt and bulky sweater. The soft green cotton sweater bore an expensive trademark across her left breast and Dan ached to trace the embroidered emblem. He stripped off his gloves and dropped them into his hat, placing it on the cheap plastic table. Paper clutter, a calculator and pieces of a broken pencil lay beneath a gooseneck lamp. He recognized the Fallcreek Bank's logo on her checkbook.

Curled on a towel near the old refrigerator, a cat yawned leisurely. Big yellow eyes stared at him until Hannah placed a bowl of milk on the floor. The cat stood, stretched in a rippling movement, then settled down to sip daintily.

Hanging his shearling coat beside her red down jacket on the wall hooks, Dan noted Else's jars of pickles and jams on the wooden shelves lining the kitchen. Stuffed with wooden spoons and utensils, a small white crock stood near the old electric stove. Hannah's peach bra and panties hung with other clothing from the old wood ladder attached to the ceiling's wooden beams. Snaring the faint light from the windows, the fuchsia and purple African violets bloomed across a battered small chest of drawers.

The plastic covering the windows fluttered in the wind as Hannah prepared coffee. He recognized the battered tin pot as Earl's.

The designer jeans fitted Hannah's hips snugly, yet Dan noted her weight loss. Padding on the scrubbed linoleum in workman's socks, she turned to him. "The wood stove is in the living room, Dan. You can stoke it up, if you want to be helpful."

He nodded, then sat and tugged off his boots. He placed them beside hers on a rug near the door.

Caught by the image of his clothing next to hers, Dan found himself crushing her red down coat. He forced his fingers to open.

Shadowy memories of Earl clung to the living room. The round, flat basket he had used to carry the chickens' grain sat on the floor, piled with colorful balls of yarn. Stacks of old frames and pictures cluttered one corner. Hannah had selected her parents' portraits for an arrangement on one wall.

Surrounded by mounds of frothy mauve and yellow chintz ruffles, an old sewing machine perched atop an oak library table that he recognized as Iris's. A clutter of scissors and threads lay in a rough wooden bowl beside it.

Dan paused, running his finger around the pioneer bread bowl and absorbing the warmth his home lacked.

She'd been sleeping on the old couch, covered by a patchwork quilt.... A crocheted maroon afghan spilled onto the scrubbed hardwood floor. A rosebud-spattered pillow still held the shape of her head and snapshots and albums lay scattered on a braided rug. Wadded tissues lay in the folds of the afghan as if she'd been crying. Dan rubbed the side of his throat, remembering Hannah's tears warming his skin....

He added wood to the cast-iron stove, then noted his mother's large walnut rocker nestled in a shadowy corner.

The runners were flattened, the wood needed sanding and varnishing. He touched the back and the rocker moved, catching on the flat places as though his mother were rocking one of her grandchildren. The rhythmic creaking caught Dan in memories until Hannah's scent stirred the air and she said quietly, "Else brought it with some things of my parents'. She said that every home needed a rocking chair. I'm going to refinish it, build up the runners and give it back.... If you've checked out the stove, let's go into the kitchen. Your coffee is ready. Then you can go."

As if reclaiming her territory, the cat leaped onto the afghan and curled into a ball, watching Dan.

Dan eased warily into the ancient wood chair at the table as Hannah leaned against the log wall, sipping her coffee. Cradled in shadows and faint light, Hannah's slender, leggy body suited the settler's house, as if she belonged in it. "There are two chairs, Smokey," he said, nodding at the empty one and pulling it out a little.

"So there are." Cradling her mug in her hand, Hannah stared out the window at the gray sky.

The old refrigerator hummed, breaking the long silence.

Dan watched the light strike her profile. What did she want? What was she thinking of? The past, the future? *Her husband? Lover? Of leaving him again?*

He stepped into the silence, slashing at it with the first words he could find. "Smart move, stacking the wood to block the wind from the house. The house has a homey feel now. Earl's wife wasn't into sewing or plants."

Her lashes flickered, a cord in her throat tightening. "Earl's wife was too sick to care about her home. My mother loved making things—sewing and knitting—and growing things."

Dan glanced into the living room and around the kitchen, wondering about her home in Seattle. "Everything is either old or new. You travel light, Smokey. Are you having your things shipped from Seattle, or won't you be here long enough?"

He wanted to know about Jordan, to know exactly how much better her husband could provide than an ex-rodeo rancher trying to keep up two ranches by day. At night he pulled on his glasses and shot holes in scripts. Occasionally he tutored an actor for authenticity, and between it all made enough to survive.

He noted the tiny empty holes in her lobes. From the day she arrived, Hannah had dismissed jewelry. Her slender ring finger was unmarked by the indentation or pale strip of a wedding band.

She ripped the rubber band from her hair and tossed it into the trash as easily as she dismissed his curiosity. Her hand swept through the thick russet strands, shaking them free. The light played on the tips and they glistened, fiery red against her pale cheek.

He wondered, then, how she would look in the dawn after a night of lovemaking.

Another man knew the answer.... Jealousy ripped through him, his fingers curling tightly around the mug as he lashed out at her. "What makes you think you can survive the winter, Smokey?"

"I will," she said quietly, her head lifting higher and leveling those stormy eyes at him. "I have to."

She'd go down fighting and could lose her life. The thought terrified him, his hands shaking. "It looks like a hard winter. The stock will have to be watered and fed, blizzard or not. If Apache spooks and you fall off, there won't be a damn person around for miles to help you. Electricity can go out, so can the phone."

"I'm getting a kerosene heater. There's plenty of wood."

Dan's fears ricocheted through him, his body tense. Had he pushed too hard, forcing her into the isolated cabin? "Hardheaded female... You were young and made a mistake, Smokey." He ran his hand across his jaw, his fingertips finding his scar and dropping away. "Back then, a lot of mistakes were made and you caught the brunt of most of them. You can't pay for your parents' mistakes with your life," he stated flatly.

She rubbed the rim of the mug across her lips thoughtfully. "I won't. I wouldn't give you the pleasure of keeping

Ferguson land." She placed her mug in the sink and walked to him, stretching out her hand. "Finished?"

The blisters on her palm had broken, angry pink patches tearing across her pale, smooth skin. Dan gripped her wrists, bringing both her hands in front of him. Before she tore her hands away, he saw a freshly healed cut blazed across the pad of her thumb; a deep infected scratch tore across the back of her left hand.

Dan rose slowly to his feet, anger ricocheting through him. He didn't want to care, but he did. Part of him remembered Else's announcement that he had always loved Hannah and the other part was furious, denying his emotions. Hannah took one step back, then another as he scowled at her. "What are you trying to prove?" he demanded, before picking her up and carrying her into the living room.

He dropped her onto the couch. "Stay there. You are going to listen to sense, if I have to make you." When she scrambled to her feet, Dan deftly wrapped the afghan around her, hampering her movements, and sat with her on his lap.

Hannah met his frown with her own, her body rigid. "You back off. You're not my keeper."

They breathed heavily, each refusing to release the stare. "Hell, you look like you're riding on a thin rail...circles under your eyes. You look like you haven't slept in weeks and you're losing weight.... You don't stand a chance," he stated finally.

"Neither do you," she returned hotly.

"Why did you cry at the Fandango? Do you miss Jordan that much?" he demanded harshly. Dan pushed hard, laying open wounds and hurting her, but he had to know. She struggled against him, and Dan's body reacted instantly, his arms tightening to still her.

He'd wanted her for years.

"Smokey..." Was that aching raw voice his own? he wondered as his fingers stroked her hot cheek.

Her eyes widened, her lips already parting for his kiss. "Dan..."

"How I've wanted you...." he whispered shakily, tugging the afghan away. Taking her hands in one of his, he kissed the wounds gently. He suckled the tip of each finger, watching her eyes darken and heat.

He placed her hand on his chest, over his heavily beating heart. He ached for her, trembling with the need to make her a part of him after all these years.

If he never held another woman in his life, he needed Hannah at this moment.

Dan breathed heavily, holding still as her fingers played with the hair on his chest. "Let me hold you like I did that night, Hannah...with nothing between us...." he asked carefully, afraid that any wrong move or word could shatter the moment. His fear swelled, swallowing him.

"Dan..." The word held an ache and a denial, her lips trembling and moist. She arched fractionally against him, the softness of her breast and hip flowing into the hard contour of his body.

His hand found the tiny buttons on the green sweater, flipping them open, one by one, as though destroying the years without her. "Don't tell me to stop," he said unevenly, knowing that with one word, Hannah could destroy him.

She stroked his taut jaw, brushing aside a strand of hair from his forehead. Then, reaching to cradle the back of his head, she brought his lips to hers.

Dan had never tasted anything so sweet, lingering in the moist, sensual brush of her lips. Her hand slid up, under his sweater and T-shirt, smoothing the hard contour of his chest and lean stomach.

For an instant, the fear within him calmed. Then another need arose too quick to be denied.

He found and caressed her breast, the tender weight fragile and silky beneath his callused hand. He had to have her breasts against his chest, stripping away their sweaters.

Dan lifted her higher, closing his eyes as her softness finally nestled against him. He trembled, heat enfolding him as he stroked her back.

He absorbed the moment, savoring the feel of her in his arms. Fearing to disturb her, fearing that she would move away, Dan breathed quietly. Hannah was the missing part of him, of his life and past, and now she had returned.

For an aeon, she lay in his arms, stroking his tense shoulders, her face hot against his throat. Dan caressed her back, sliding his fingers beneath the jeans to stroke the silky smooth curve of her hips. His fingers tangled in a lace confection and wanting nothing between them, he tore it away, cupping her as he levered his legs up on the couch.

Lying over him, Hannah kissed a trail to his ear, nibbling on it while he held his breath, afraid the miracle of holding Hannah would evaporate with the next fiery burst of pine pitch.

She came at him then, winding him.

Her teeth caught his nipple, worrying it as her hand found him, stroking him urgently.

Dan inhaled sharply, caught by the sudden blazing hunger. In the next moment, her jeans lay on the floor, her soft limbs moving urgently against him.

"Hannah, sweet Hannah...wait...." Dan surged against the brush of her hand, the intensity rocking him.

Hannah ignited in his arms. "Now...oh, my darling, now..."

Breathing hard, Dan hunted desperately for a measure of sanity. Then Hannah moved urgently against him and his last hold on reality flew into the December wind. She fumbled with his belt and jeans and Dan shifted to help her, realizing distantly that she was inexperienced in undressing a man.

Then Hannah's long legs were creamy smooth and warm on his, when his jeans slid to the floor.

Straining to make the moment last, Dan tumbled Hannah to the floor, wrapped in his arms, the afghan and blanket. Leaning over her, trembling with the need to enter her, Dan placed his elbows beside her head. He smoothed her hair away from her face, studying the wild disarray, to lock her in his memories. "Not this way, Hannah. Not fast," he managed, despite the fever racking him.

He wanted to make long, sweet love to her. To show her with his body how much he cared. To prove to her that what they had would last and last.... To set the pace that would bind her to him.

Then she moved, crying out to him. "Oh, Dan, I need you so.... Help me...."

Her body moved fluidly, cupping his in a soft tangle of arms and thighs and sweet, hungry kisses.

"Hannah...I don't have anything..." Then the tip of his fullness rested against her intimately, and Dan forgot everything but needing Hannah.

He hurt her at first and she stiffened, crying out softly. Poised just that bit inside her moist warmth, Dan closed his eyes, forcing himself to wait. "Hannah, honey...wait. You're...too tight," he whispered against her ear, smoothing her hair. "Honey, wait..."

Shivering with desire, Hannah's dark gray eyes lifted to his. Her arms wrapped around him, holding him tight. And then he saw the wild fear binding her. Dan kissed her cheek, her damp lashes and the tip of her nose. "Wait, honey...just wait."

He stroked her breasts, watching his tanned hands encompass the delicate softness. "Easy, honey..." he urged, bending to suckle the dark rose tip.

A drop of sweat ran down his throat with the effort of holding himself from her.

Hannah trembled beneath him, her body taut. She frowned, biting her lips as she looked away from him. "It's been a long time...."

Turning her chin with his finger, Dan kissed her gently. "I know... I haven't had a woman for years.... It's been forever."

She lay looking up at him, soft and needing. "I don't know what to do...."

"You're doing everything perfect, honey," Dan murmured, noting the flow of her body beneath his hand. "You're where you belong.... With me."

He grinned then. "You know I feel like a boy with his first girl. Trying to size up the situation, and not too certain how to do it. Blaylock men are noted for—" he entered a bit farther and her eyes widened "—for that...."

Recognizing his attempt to help her, Hannah smiled slowly, a sensuous warmth rippling through her. "Are you boasting, Blaylock?"

"Could be." He slid his hand down her body, spanning the soft warmth low on her stomach and rubbing it. "Are you still hurting?"

She trailed a fingertip down to his nipple, toying with it. Dan stiffened immediately, sliding into her. He tensed, feeling the first contractions ripple through her immediately. Sheathed deeply in her, Dan knew that this time was for her and fought his passion. Lying beneath him tautly, Hannah closed her eyes and he sensed her drawing into herself, savoring the intensity of her desire. Her gray eyes opened suddenly, staring up at him questioningly.

Fighting the need to find his own desire, Dan kissed her hard on the mouth. "Having fun?" he asked tenderly.

"I..." she began, raising her hips to his. Then she nipped his shoulder; the small pain sent him surging deeper.

"Hannah," he warned roughly. "You're asking for trouble."

She kissed the small wound, then stroked it with the tip of her tongue. "You taught me how to ride, Dan. This can't be that much different. Unless you're too old to keep up."

Dan lifted an eyebrow. "Honey, we're playing games without protection...." Then Hannah raised her hips, tugging him deeper and he groaned, shaking in her arms as the fever swept over him.

She cried out then, gathering him deeper. "Love me, Dan. Love me.... I have to know...."

I have to know.... The words echoed in Dan's mind later as he cradled Hannah's sleeping body against him.

You taught me how to ride.... He tugged the blanket over her bare shoulder and watched the early afternoon light drift through the windowpane.

I have to know.... You taught me how to ride.... Hannah's slender hand caressed his bare chest slowly and she mumbled his name in her sleep, nuzzling her cheek against his shoulder.

Dan listened to the refrigerator humming and a cow calling her calf and thought about Hannah. She acted as if he were her first lover—tutoring her body to each new caress, startled when he surged against her a second time. Laughing in delight before she kissed him hungrily. "Oh, Dan...I never knew."

Oh, Dan...I never knew. Filled with wonder and excitement, Hannah's husky voice echoed around him as she snuggled closer.

Locked in his desire, struggling to prolong the endless sweet moment of her body joined to his, Dan had whispered something rawly. He searched for the elusive words now as Hannah sighed. She slept deeply and he knew it would be hours before she awoke. He lingered in the soft drape of limbs and scents, wanting to wake her and love again. What had he whispered?

Perched on the back of the couch, the cat returned his stare.

Hannah had cried out, the soft tone filled with awe as he loved her.

He loved her. Dan closed his eyes, recalling the ultimate moment when he'd whispered the words. His desperation had matched her own, their hunger poised on the pinnacle of fulfillment.

I didn't know.... Hannah's husky, drowsy whisper filled his memory.

The cat blinked and Dan nuzzled Hannah's fragrant hair. Whatever had happened between them was deeper than the immediate hunger.

That night Hannah lay on the couch, watching the flickering flames and thinking of Dan. She'd awakened slowly to his scent, the tension that ran through her body for years eased by the full sensation of his loving. She yawned and stretched leisurely, aching pleasantly in every muscle. She'd put off rising from the floor, snuggling to the warmth she'd shared with Dan. In the early evening she checked on the stock and noted that Dan had repaired the barn roof despite her objections.

In the house, she had stoked the fire and returned to the couch, wrapping herself in the memories of their lovemaking.

Her parents' portraits, all three of them, drew her gaze and she knew what Iris had found with Earl. The sharing, the stark desire to be a part of her lover. The tenderness and the fire and the hunger to begin anew . . .

Ethan's tender and methodic lovemaking lay in shreds after Dan's fiery response to her needs. Then Dan wanted more, feeding on their hunger a second time. In comparison, Ethan's lovemaking was a surface emotion . . . a passing, placid moment of caring, neatly tucked away.

Hannah shivered, licking her swollen, well-kissed lips. Dan's lovemaking was a storm. Fever hot, then tender and sharing. Amid the tempest, did Dan whisper, "I love you"? Or did her dreams of long ago echo through her passion?

Running the flat of her hand down her body, she thought of Dan's head resting on her breast. Vulnerable in the aftermath of lovemaking, Dan had held her tightly, as though he feared losing her. His lashes were suddenly damp on her skin; the moment sweet as she caressed his trembling shoulders and soothed him with soft, lingering kisses.

She moved against the back of the couch, needing a security like Dan's hard warmth, and closed her eyes.

Whatever the fever to love Dan was, she would find the cure. *Daniel Blaylock was not wounding her a second time.*

Dan used Melissa's letter to mark his place in the script, then leaned back in his easy chair, staring at the snowflakes sliding from the night to hit his windows. His empty house creaked around him like the memories of loving Hannah. He'd turned every facet of the morning around for hours, treasuring every soft, hungry touch. . . . "Smokey . . ." he whispered to the empty shadows, aching for her.

Every instinct he possessed told him one thing: *He was Smokey's first real lover.*

He'd give her time to work out her past. Dan reached to pick up the telephone and dialed Hannah. After a moment, she answered sleepily, reminding him of her drowsy protest when he had left her side earlier. "Are you okay?" he asked huskily.

"Go 'way, Daniel Blaylock," she muttered sleepily before the line clicked into a dead hum.

Dan smiled grimly and replaced the phone. "Not likely, Miss Hannah. Not until I'm finished. Before then, you're going to tell me a few things."

His gaze skipped to the framed pictures of the numerous Blaylock children, sprayed across his mantel. Years ago he'd wanted a family with Hannah and now she could be carrying his son.

The image ricocheted through the empty house, keeping the arctic wind and time at bay. His child resting in Hannah's arms....

Dan settled deeper in his chair, watching the snow hit the windows and slide away, like the years.

Whatever Jordan had shared with Hannah, she was startled by her passion, experiencing the limits of hunger and fire for the first time.

Dan inhaled deeply, locking the knowledge within him. Whatever happened between them in the future, he'd touched Hannah in a way that no other man had. For the time, that was enough.

Six

———

Hannah snuggled deeper beneath the blankets and afghan. Gertrude padded slowly down her hips, then eased into the back of Hannah's knees. The tantalizing aroma of freshly brewed coffee drifted before Hannah's sleepy senses. She dozed for a long luxurious moment, sighing as a persistent nudge bothered her feet. She moved her toes slightly and the nudge followed. "Scat," she grumbled sleepily. "Your milk can wait."

Tucked behind her knees, Gertrude purred loudly and in the distance, a slow, rhythmic creak sounded. The nudge slowly, steadily worked up to her calf. The fire crackled, burning as though it had just been stoked and the aroma of coffee—coffee?

Hannah opened her eyes slowly. Dan sat in his mother's rocker, his feet propped up on the couch and sharing the quilts with her. "Dan!"

He sipped the coffee, then cradled the mug in his hands as he leaned against the rocker back, his eyes closed. In a dark red wool shirt and worn jeans, Dan presented the picture of a relaxed, comfortable male lounging in a familiar room ... with a familiar woman, one to whom he had just made deep, satisfying love. Every nerve in Hannah's body tightened and a sudden deep ache shot through her, reminding her of Dan's body melding with hers in a fiery heat that became a tender glow. His stocking-covered toes caressed her ankle. "Hmm?"

Hannah sat up, clutching the folds of the quilt to her chest with trembling fingers. *"What are you doing here?"*

"Drinking coffee," he answered lazily, a strand of hair crossing his forehead. He hadn't shaved, the dark stubble giving him a rakish look. "Else sent some yeast rolls. They're hot and buttered. Want one?"

Hannah threw the edge of the quilt over her shoulder. Sheathed in her thermal underwear, she needed all the protection possible against Dan. *"Why...are...you...here?"* she asked, trying desperately to place her thoughts in a straight line. Dan's big body and sexy, rumpled, lovable image kept interfering. Her fingers crushed the quilt, remembering the masculine texture flowing beneath them as they made love.

Dan rocked slowly, the chair creaking under his heavy weight. "Delivering Else's rolls."

"Dan..." Hannah began huskily. "You keep your distance. You can't turn up here at dawn—"

He chuckled, a full rich sound, and stretched lazily. "Try ten o'clock. Else called me at six to pick up her rolls. I've done my chores and yours, heated up those rolls in the oven. And it's a little late to tell me to keep my distance."

With shaking fingers, Hannah reached for the mug of steaming coffee placed on a stack of catalogs. She cradled it in her hands, sipping the hot brew and fighting to remain calm. Dan's toes toyed with hers leisurely and she drew them away. The rocker continued to creak slowly. Dan rocked as though he had all the time in the world.

Yesterday morning's passion lay between them, hotter than the coffee they now shared. "If you came over here to gloat, Daniel Josiah Blaylock, do it and get out," she ordered, running a trembling hand through her tangled hair.

"There won't be a second helping and you're not using yesterday as leverage to pry me off Ferguson land."

His lids opened slowly, the thick, sooty lashes barely revealing the glitter in his eyes. "Drink that coffee, Smokey. Maybe it will sweeten that hellcat mood. Jordan may have put up with it, but I won't."

"Hellcat!" she sputtered, glaring at him. "Now there's a macho definition...."

"There's not a prescription in the kitchen or bathroom, and not in your pretty little, expensive, handmade Italian purse. I could be a daddy next year," he stated flatly. "Haven't forgotten the necessities before this ... Since it's my first possibility of a child, I'd like to know. Gives a man an immortal edge on life, having a family. Now I know how my brothers felt when their women were expecting."

For a moment, Hannah's lips moved silently. Shaking with anger, she demanded, "What right do you have prowling through my things?"

Dan lifted a heavy eyebrow at her, the scar ricocheting down his cheek. The meaningful stare held her as a blush rose slowly up her throat to tint her cheeks. "You've been sleeping hard. I've been here an hour, waiting for you to wake. Did you find out what you wanted to know?" he asked without moving.

I have to know, she remembered in a stark glimpse of holding him tight and seeking the ultimate, shattering fulfillment that she had never experienced with Ethan. *Why did she have to react to Dan with that fiery, desperate hunger?*

In a long length of worn jeans, his coffee mug resting atop his flat waist, Dan Blaylock would wait forever for an answer.

"You don't have to worry about fathering a child with me, Dan. There, now you can get out."

"Why haven't you had children, Smokey?" he pushed softly, slowly sitting upright. He placed his mug on the floor and stood to his full height over her. A square of dim morning light slid from the window to frame his big body, blocking out everything else in the room. In that moment,

Dan looked as tough and unmoving as his ancestors. He rubbed his palm over his scar, long legs locked into an easy stance. His hard lips barely moved, as he threw questions at her. "Didn't want them? Didn't want strings to Jordan? Is something physically wrong with you? What?" His intensity slammed her back against the couch.

Dan bent quickly, framing her face with his callused hands and drawing it to his. His thumbs traced her cheekbones, his long, lean fingers spearing into her hair. "Damn, you're beautiful in the morning," he whispered huskily, before kissing her with an intensity that made her forget everything else. The hunger and desire lasted when he stood, looking down at her darkly. "Don't look so panicked, Smokey," he said softly. "Everyone comes full circle once in their life. If there's a baby, I'd like that."

Then he was gone, leaving her lips tender and aching. Particles of dust and time circled the sunlight passing into the room as Hannah stared at her mother's portrait. She brushed her fingertips across her mouth, tasting Dan's hungry kiss. "Is this how you felt, Mother?"

She lay back, sipping her coffee and thinking about Dan. "He doesn't play fair," she muttered finally, taking one of Else's rolls to her mouth.

Dan had buttered and spread jam across the roll. Gertrude's milk bowl crashed and a sleepy big-boned puppy lumbered into the room, all brown fur and big, wary black eyes. He began yipping at Gertrude, who arched her back and hissed.

Later Hannah found a note with Dan's bold scrawl tucked inside her folded bra and panties on the table. "Pup is out of James's watchdog. Has all his shots. I'll take him when you leave."

She crumpled the note and scooped up the squirming puppy in her arms. "When I leave," she repeated darkly, twisting away from the puppy's licking tongue and scratching his ears. "You can wait until cows fly, Dan Blaylock. You couldn't pry me off Ferguson land with a crowbar."

At noon, Hannah parked Jessie in front of the home in which she'd grown up. Sally and Jimmy Demornay had purchased the old two-story white house, maintaining it with fresh paint and a modern addition to the kitchen. The sprawling wide porch and massive pillars stood above the snow, reminding her of long hours spent reading teen magazines and gossiping with her friends.

Sally opened the massive oak door with a grin. "About time," she said, hugging Hannah's shoulders. "Jimmy and I bought the place after... after your father passed away. I hope you like the changes we've made. We've added on to the kitchen, of course, and changed the old fixtures." She took Hannah's down coat and hung it in the closet. "Would you like something to eat before we begin? Oh, I'm so excited. Else and Bernadette say you are doing marvelous at Earl's place. They say the rustic country look is just perfect for that homestead. Imagine... a real interior decorator," she beamed at Hannah, who returned the smile warmly.

"I've just begun. There will be plenty of time this winter. I'm anxious to get started, but I'd love to see what you've done with the rest of the house." The refurnished house reached out to her, tossing memories at her in every room. Sally's sewing-room clutter was the same as Hannah's mother's, plants catching every bit of window light and colorful thread and material tumbling everywhere.

"This is the room I thought might do well." With a slight blush, Sally opened the door to the room that had been Hannah's nursery and playroom. "We'll lock it, of course, so the grandchildren won't be shocked," she whispered, grinning. "It's great having you back. Maude Jenkins says there's a bet in town about who will ask you out first. Then there's another bet about what Dan will do about it, if Mike or one of the other unmarried guys asks you. Else told the ladies' sewing circle that it's just a matter of time before you wear the Blaylock name. Or Dan's wedding ring. She's saved her mother's for Dan's wife."

Hannah studied the stark, clean room and the polished hardwood floors. "Dan is not my type," she said. *If there's a baby, I'd like that....*

She closed her eyes, forcing Dan's exquisite lovemaking aside. "I think dark red satin ruffles on a big brass bed, with plenty of mirrors and a shaggy white area rug under the bed.'' She glanced at the small walk-in closet. ''With a little effort, you and Jimmy could have a wonderful sexy bathroom—you know, a large corner tub with water jets...''

''Wow! Go for it.'' Sally looked at the room, her eyes widening. ''I want this room ... to make a statement like your fandango with Dan.... A statement like passion, love, romance, steam. At the same time...tender, you know? As though it was solid and would last forever. I'll never forget that dance as long as I live. I want Jimmy to feel that way about me now.''

By three o'clock, Hannah had measured the room's dimensions and laid out her plans for Sally's red-hot Jimmy-capturing boudoir. Chatting happily, Sally served tea in the kitchen and potted herbs for Hannah's home. ''I just love the smell of herbs growing in the kitchen. The fresh taste is marvelous.''

Hannah turned the clay pot of chives. ''I've always wanted to try growing them.''

Sally beamed. ''In the spring, I'll dig up tarragon and lavender starts for your garden.''

On the drive home Hannah passed the local cemetery, pulling her truck off the side of the road. She had avoided visiting her parents' graves, but something drew her to them now.

Covered with a blanket of snow, the resting places of her family lay within a small wrought-iron fence. The wind swept through the pine boughs as she stood there, wrapped in her thoughts and the swirling snowflakes.

Suddenly Dan stood behind her, his arms gathering her close as he rocked her. ''They'd want you to be happy,'' he whispered roughly against her ear as she began to cry.

She struggled against his strength for a moment, sobbing. ''Go 'way, Daniel Blaylock.''

Instead he drew her nearer, turning her to him and sheltering her body in the hard length of his. ''It'll work out, Smokey,'' he said, tucking her face against his throat. ''You're tough. You'll see it through.''

"Not with you," she managed, after a moment in which she couldn't force herself to move away from Dan's warmth into the winter wind.

Dan's kiss brushed her temple, his strong fingers seeking the taut cords at the back of her neck and massaging them. "Take your time, Smokey," he said gently, rocking her against him. "Work it out."

The second week of December, Galahad, Hannah's puppy, chewed her handmade Italian purse to shreds. Doug Fallcreek placed a deposit to redecorate the bank in Hannah's account.

The Demornays became Jasmine's hottest gossip item. The post-office clerk confided about the mysterious packages destined to the Demornays to the catalog-ordering clerk, who whispered about the sexy see-through nightie Sally had ordered ... with bikini panties. Jimmy Demornay ordered a fantastic sound system and seemed years younger. Sally ordered Jimmy a short satin men's robe and black bikini underwear when she ordered her new push-up bra. Strangely marked boxes addressed to the Demornays arrived at the post office and they uninvited their children for New Year's Eve. Jimmy called a neighbor to move his stock into another pasture, saying he was "too tuckered to toot." There was talk of a second honeymoon in Paris. Evelyn Throckmorton decided that Jimmy had strayed and Sally was making sure it didn't happen a second time. Mort Raznick thought Sally might be looking for middle-aged excitement with another man and Jimmy was putting an end to it.

Twice in the next week Hannah awoke at dawn to Galahad's wild barking and Big Al's bellowing. When she ran to the window, Dan was in the feedlot tending cattle.

Dan called her periodically at night, his deep voice rasping across her skin. She slept on the couch, snuggling against the firm back, though she'd managed to clean and finish one bedroom.

Else called to chat and managed to convey the message that her little brother needed a woman's firm hand if he wasn't to die on the range, his life wasted and empty behind him.

During the days, Hannah renailed the loose boards on the large loafing shed that sheltered the stock from winter blizzards. Big Al kept her company, snorting steam into the clear, cold air and ignoring Galahad's antics in the snow. Macedonia allowed her to sit with him in the barn, a friend from long ago. In the afternoons she sketched designs for the bank and telephoned for wallpaper and fabric swatches.

Then there were the long evenings working in the house, and when Hannah was too tired to move she lay staring at her parents' portraits, unraveling the mystery of her birth. When she finally slept, she dreamed of Dan's tender lovemaking and awoke to find herself trembling, aching for his strong arms. Their lovemaking had erupted out of a desperate, poignant need lying dormant for years. Their sweet passion had been brief, yet she would carry the memory into eternity. *Why hadn't she experienced the physical heights with Ethan? Or the reverent spiritual bonding on that high, shimmering plateau? As though she was a part of Dan and he was one with her?*

The day came when she knew there would be no child, and though she knew she couldn't conceive, she ached with emptiness instead of relief. Blaylock children were beautiful and deeply loved by an extensive family circle.

Christmas week, Else asked her to attend the Blaylock Christmas dinner to be held in the town hall. That same night, Mike asked her to a New Year's Eve dinner and dancing at Jasmine's only café and tavern.

The Blaylock family potluck dinner encompassed the elderly to the last eight-month-old Blaylock baby. Else placed Dan next to Hannah, with the expertise of an accomplished society hostess. Dan slid into the seat next to her, his plate filled high from the potluck buffet. He lifted his cup of punch to toast her, his black eyes gleaming.

Dressed in charcoal slacks and a dark red sweater, Dan's big body leaned next to hers, brushing her shoulder as he reached for the salt and pepper. The tantalizing scent of soap and male swirled around Hannah as she pushed her food with her fork, trying to ignore all six foot four, two hundred plus pounds of appealing, dominating, exasperating male.

"I like the pink lace dress," he drawled, regarding the old-fashioned dress she'd found at a thrift shop. With a high neck and long, puffy sleeves, the dress needed little altering to fit Hannah's slender waist, and seemed perfect for the Christmas dinner. The heat in Dan's eyes caused her to remember how he had looked at her during their lovemaking. As though he wanted to consume her on the spot. As though he'd wrap her in love and tenderness until the end of time.

He studied her mother's locket, suspended from a black ribbon against her throat. The gold heart lay over the transparent pink lace bodice above the champagne slip. Dan studied the feminine contours until her breasts thrust against the cloth, then he followed the length of her throat to her lips. The look of controlled hunger held until Hannah nervously slid the tip of her tongue across her lips, moistening them.

"Can't you find someplace else to sit?" she asked quietly. "The gossip is thick enough already."

He considered the thought while eating Else's cranberry-and-orange salad. "Sure is," he answered easily, not moving an inch. "How are you?" The intimate low tone brought her head pivoting toward him.

She fought the blush rising up her throat and found Dan's gaze on her breasts again. "I'm not pregnant, if that's what you mean," she whispered desperately.

Dan lowered his gaze to his cup of punch, his expression hardening. A vein in his tanned, muscled throat throbbed heavily and his fingers tightened on the cup. It shattered, exploding red punch and glass across the white tablecloth.

Else was there instantly, cleaning the table. "They don't make punch cups like they used to," she murmured, sliding the cup's handle off Dan's finger and dusting his palm for glass.

His hard stare never left Hannah's taut expression as Else slipped another punch cup near him and vanished. "Too bad, princess. I had hopes," he said finally, when Missy Blaylock climbed onto his knee.

The little girl curled her arm around Dan's shoulders and held a sprig of mistletoe over his head. She rubbed her nose to his and lisped, "Kiss me, Uncle Dan. I caught you. Mommy said you were taking us kids on a sleigh ride with a marshmallow bonfire."

He grinned, suddenly looking rakish and appealing. "Is that so, buttercup? I'll kiss you and give you a quarter for that mistletoe, how about that?"

Then Missy was running to sit on Santa's lap and Dan was reaching for Hannah, drawing her to her feet.

Hannah glimpsed Else's beaming smile as she held the mistletoe over Dan's black head. Then there was Dan, dragging her close to him, his hard body pressing into the folds of pink lace as he bent her over his arm.

Hannah almost slid down to the floor beneath the sweet, hungry caress of his lips. Then Dan eased her upright, steadied her by her arm and shot her a purely arrogant, possessive male stare as the room began to focus beyond his broad shoulders. "There," he said. "You'll do."

Then she was standing alone, shivering and watching Dan pick up a year-old toddler, cuddling the boy as if the mind-drugging kiss had never happened. Hannah's heart began to beat with a dull, angry throb. Dan had just kissed her hungrily, then had turned and walked away. Her fists clenched the pale lace, when they wanted to strangle his thick neck. Holding the boy in the crook of his arm, Dan shot her another high-headed, arrogant stare beneath his sooty lashes.

"That man," Hannah muttered, smoothing her dress with unsteady hands. Dan had decided to play games in front of his family, had he? She swore that before the night was over, she would return the favor.

The adults and children caroled and exchanged presents and Dan sat beside her, his thigh hard against hers. "You're crowding me, Blaylock," she hissed, easing away.

"I intend to, Miss Hannah. It's driving me crazy just thinking of what you're wearing beneath that thing," he returned in an aside whisper just before five-year-old Jennifer came to stand between his knees.

"Uncle Dan, Grandma said you'd help me with this, that she was too busy serving cake. It's from Santa Claus. I got a brand new brush, too." The girl held out a package of elastic bands in an assortment of colors with matching satin bows. Dan took the miniature brush in his hand and propped the girl up on his knee.

Dan's work-scarred and callused fingers neatly parted Jennifer's thick length of glossy black hair down the center and began braiding it deftly. After attaching the elastic bands to the tips of her braids, Dan received a hug and a kiss. The little girl preened, turning around in her layers of ruffles and fluttering her lashes at him. "Am I pretty, Uncle Dan?"

He chuckled and lifted her up for another kiss. "Pretty as a picture." Jennifer beamed at him and Hannah's heart skipped a beat. Clearly Dan could affect feminine hearts of any age.

Emily Blaylock, another niece of Dan's, slipped an eight-month-old boy into his lap and placed a diaper bag at his boots. "Brent needs changing. I have to make more punch. Can you...?"

Hannah almost laughed as Dan stared at Emily, his lips firmly pressed together as if keeping an oath back. "Why me?" he demanded in a growling tone between his teeth. "I've changed Brent more than you have. You're his mother." But he was already reaching for the diaper bag.

Unscathed by his remark, Emily bent to kiss and pat his cheek. "Mothers need helping hands," she quoted sweetly, fluttering her lashes at him. "Thanks, Uncle Dan," she said, before swishing into the kitchen.

Dan mumbled something about mothers taking care of the backsides of their children, as he neatly changed the diaper and flopped a clean one over his broad shoulder. He lifted the baby against him and rubbed his back expertly as Hannah began to smile. He shot her an ominous stare as the baby explored his ear. "Don't say a word."

She laughed outright and his scowl deepened.

Hannah helped the Blaylock women later, pouring coffee and serving cake, while the male members sat apart and talked intently.

Emily nudged Hannah's shoulder. "It's the Blaylock powwow. Women are excluded. They talk about tractors, crops, that sort of thing. Oh, then there's hunting and fishing. Grandma used to say that it comes from the Apache and Spanish blood and pure male arrogance that needed to be cut down a notch. She said it took a good woman to match a Blaylock man, one who could be tough and ease their pain when they ached. Blaylock men weren't bred to be sweethearts, that's for certain. Trimming off those rough edges can be downright exciting."

She winked and grinned. "So we leave them alone and let them think they're still ruling the countryside."

When Hannah bent near Dan's shoulder to lift and fill his coffee cup, her breast brushed his shoulder. She hesitated, caught by the swirling need to stroke the back of his tense, proud head and smooth the crisp, raven hair. Dan tensed, looking straight ahead.

She returned the cup to its place and his arm moved slightly, brushing the outer perimeter of her breast again. He breathed slowly, stirring his coffee. "Could use some more. You barely filled the cup," he murmured, sitting straighter.

Hannah couldn't resist paying him back for that devastating kiss. Taking her time, she bent near him, repeating the task. "My cup was on the other side. Put it back," he ordered, flicking a taunt at her through his lashes.

Taking a deep, steadying breath, Hannah met his challenge, her breast brushing his cheek. His reaction was just what she wanted, a quick intake of breath, his scar shifting as though he gritted his teeth.

Dan turned slowly to stare at her. "You're pushing your luck, Smokey," he drawled. "Of course, we could step outside to finish this one-up fandango...."

A Blaylock male's disgruntled tone slid between them. "Women. There's no peace."

Dan held her eyes, then he took the coffeepot to place it on the table. His fingers locked around her wrist, his thumb smoothing the soft inner flesh. He tugged slightly. "Sit down. You're not going anywhere."

The muscles sliding across his jaw tensed, his gaze challenging her. As though a single body, the Blaylock women inhaled and stared at Dan's dark fingers wrapped around Hannah's pale wrist. Their collective gaze swung from Dan's determined expression to Hannah's proud one and returned.

The Blaylock men shot ominous glares at Hannah and at the women. A teenage male snorted in disgust. In the distance, Missy Blaylock's childish voice asked, "Mommy? Why can't we sit at the powwow table, too?"

Then Jake Tallman, a Blaylock cousin, rose slowly to his feet. Chairs scooted back as Dan and twenty-six tall, rugged Blaylock men rose to their feet, waiting for Hannah to sit. Jake eased aside his six-foot-three frame to allow space for her.

Dan's expression tossed a dark, simmering challenge at her. Taking it, she sat beside Dan, her shoulders brushing his arm. The tall men sat, chairs scraped as they got comfortable and the steady drone of masculine voices continued. As Dan talked with the other men, he caressed her wrist and drew her hand to his thigh beneath the table. His muscles hardened beneath the slack material and he glanced down at her with arrogance and possession.

An image flashed in Hannah's mind, that of a proud warrior's woman, kept at his side to serve him and one whom he cherished above all other women.

But there was a tender pride, and a need that matched her own to be close to him. That held her until he released her hand moments later.

Dan sipped hot chocolate and studied Hannah's photograph from the dinner, Else's gift to him. Hannah looked hot and bothered just after that kiss, a strand of dark red hair resting on the pink lace bodice. He tracked the row of tiny buttons on the photo, imagining the silky skin beneath. He rubbed the rim of his mug across his lips, thinking of Hannah's mouth parting, warming and answering.

In the next minute, three other Blaylock men had hooted
and grabbed their wives to apply the same, love-me-forever
kiss. Else had captured the moment with an instant photo,
catching each of the Blaylock women with a drowsy, sensual expression of what-hit-me?

Dan ran his thumb over the glossy surface of the snap-
shot and leaned back in his chair, propping his boots on the
worn chair opposite his computer. The frothy lace confection swirling around Hannah's long, smooth legs had raised
his temperature the moment she walked into the town hall
carrying a casserole. For whatever time Hannah spent in the
valley before she ran off again, she was his.

*The next time they made love, it would take days, not
hours*. Dan rubbed his flat stomach, soothing the ache
burning there. Those fleeting hours had left him with a huge
appetite for Hannah's pale skin.

He toyed with his mother's wedding ring on the tip of his
little finger for a moment, then turned back to the computer, set his glasses in place and began entering his cri-
tique of the Western's showdown scene. In another fifteen
minutes, he clicked off the computer, tossed the glasses aside
and picked up the phone to call Hannah.

Every male instinct he possessed sharpened at the sleepy,
husky sound of her voice when she answered. "Smokey,"
he said, picturing her body curving beneath the long thermal underwear...picturing the delicate shades of her breasts
and the pale smooth expanse of her skin. "I'll pick you up
for Mamie's New Year's Eve party at six."

"Really?" she asked after a moment, her voice sounding
more awake.

He grinned at the saucy tone. Smokey wouldn't make
anything easy on him. "Really."

"Can't."

Her smug tone evoked a picture of a cat purring on a
sunny windowsill...after eating the canary. Dan sat upright, his eyes narrowing. "Fine. We'll spend New Year's
Eve here or at your place."

"Can't."

He pictured her saucy grin. Dan strangled the receiver. "Why the hell not?"

Hannah laughed, a long sultry, I've-got-you-now sound. "Because I have other plans. By the way, the next time you grab me, you snake, watch out."

"You terrify me," he returned flatly. "I'll pick you up at six."

"I have other plans."

Dan thought about ripping the telephone from the wall. "Change them," he ordered curtly.

She laughed softly. "Can't. See you around."

On New Year's Eve, Hannah enjoyed Mike's company over a steak-and-baked-potato dinner at Mamie's Café and Tavern. Easy-going Mike did wonders for her ego, performing a long, low wolf whistle at her form-fitting jeans and tailored cobalt-blue Western-style blouse. Embroidered flowers flowed down the long sleeves; the blouse had been a gift from a pleased customer in Seattle. "You look great, Hannah," he said when she laughed outright. "Want to try out the dance floor?"

Jack's Country Band played cajun, Western and country rock, delighting the customers. Periodically a young singer with long hair and earrings stepped up to the microphone to deliver a throbbing love song. Waltzing and two-stepping with Mike, Hannah relaxed for the first time in years. Mike twirled her, danced close with her and the years slipped away. "You're good," he said above the loud music.

She grinned up at him. "You're easy to follow. I'm having a great time, Mike. Thanks."

Two Blaylock brothers and their wives cleared the floor with a foursome dance, and James winked at her over Bernadette's head.

At eleven o'clock, Mamie's passed out noise makers and party hats. At eleven-fifteen, Dan eased through the slow dancers to Mike's side, tapping him on the shoulder.

Dressed in jeans and a plaid Western shirt that clung to his wide shoulders, Dan glanced at Hannah. Then he surveyed the dance floor as if he'd just woken up in the middle of it.

Wearing a grease smudge on his forehead, a lipstick impression of lips on his cheek and a scowl, Dan presented the image of a harried, angry man.

He looked at her pale hand resting on Mike's shoulder. The gaze slid down to Mike's hand on her waist. "I've just spent two hours pulling your ex-wife's car out of a snowdrift. She's with a state patrolman, filling out an accident report at your office." Dan's tone portrayed a wounded grizzly confronting his victim.

Mike's eyes widened. "Annie?"

Dan's gaze slid down Hannah's long legs and then lifted to her face, tracing the light application of cosmetics. "Ann's pretty badly shaken up."

Mike frowned at Hannah, and she said, "I'll find a way home."

"I'll take her. Go on, Mike," Dan added softly, already drawing Hannah into his arms.

She tried to force a distance between them with stiff arms and elbows, but Dan held her close, his lips against her forehead. His hand flattened against her back, pressing her against him. "Stay put. I'm not a happy man right now."

Ron Levy tapped Dan on the shoulder, then backed away as Dan leveled a stare at him.

Hannah couldn't help smiling serenely. "Busy night?"

"Hell, yes." He drew her closer and inhaled on a sigh. "You'd better make it up to me."

"Really? I don't know why." She decided to let Dan wear the grease smudge and lipstick and the frown. Then he kissed her forehead, nuzzling her hair, and sighed deeply again, running his hand down her back. His sigh was the sound of a cowboy finding a soft, warm place in an evil, trying world after a shootout.

They moved smoothly to the slow waltz and Hannah's cheek brushed Dan's shoulder. His scent swirled around her, and she fought the urge to move against him, holding her back very stiff. Dan's hand slid slowly down to her waist, his other hand drawing hers behind his back. "I'm not a happy man right now, Miss Hannah," he whispered against her forehead. "Mike was damn lucky."

James's broad shoulder brushed Dan's, rocking Bernadette slowly to the music as he spoke to Dan. "Heard you also took Pam to have her babies. What did she have?"

Dan grinned broadly. "Twins. Red-headed females. Weighed in at five and a half pounds apiece. Ugly as Kenny."

"Twins! A pair of red-headed great-nieces," James exclaimed, his grin matching Dan's. "How's Pam?"

"She's crying for the navy to send Kenny home from overseas. I just got her to the county hospital in time. She wouldn't let go of my hand. Almost broke it in the pickup when we ran into a drift. Macy Doolittle pulled us out with his eighteen-wheeler. For a time, I thought I'd be delivering the twins."

"Whew. For a minute when the ambulance said they couldn't make it through the drifts, I thought Else would send me to pick up Pam. So I told her you didn't have anything to do and Bernadette was counting on me tonight—"

Dan looked down at Hannah. "Thanks for the help with my life.... I had plenty to do. This one has decided to stir Mike up."

James laughed as Hannah gritted her teeth. "Looks like Miss Hannah's not that happy about being here with you."

"She's just mad because I didn't show up sooner. She missed me." Dan swirled Hannah under his arm and tucked her in close against him, his hand low on her hips.

She eased it away, narrowing her eyes at him. As if drawn to the soft curve, Dan's palm curved on her hip. "You've had a busy night," she hissed as he turned and her breasts pressed hard against his chest. "I won't keep you."

"Nice jeans," he said, fingers caressing the fabric. "Always have appreciated a woman who could wear her jeans right."

"You're holding me too tight, Dan," she said, frowning up at him. "I can date whoever I want. You may lord over Ferguson stock and land, but you don't have rights to choose whomever I date."

A muscle in Dan's jaw contracted as he gritted his teeth. His fingers slid low on her hip, drawing her against him.

"The way I see it, you're not sliding out of my bed one day and dating someone else the next."

"Your bed. A momentary weakness and you think you have rights," she hissed, stiffening as he drew her closer.

Holding her against him, Dan bent to nibble her ear and her head went up in surprise. "Weakness or not, can't say I've ever had a woman come at me that way." He turned her suddenly, inserting his hard thigh between the soft length of hers. "As if she wanted me more than air. The heat melting her silky skin until it burned me."

Hannah's gray eyes darkened. "You've made love before."

He chuckled, kissing her parted lips. "Honey, not like that. With you poured into me like warm honey. From the feel of things, you haven't ever made love like that. The next time, I'm going to love you senseless and then love you some more," he said, as the crowd began counting down the midnight hour.

"Dan..." she began, as he stroked her cheek with the tip of his finger.

"Dan..." she protested softly, as he lifted her chin, his eyes glowing.

At midnight, Dan's lips settled down on hers, an achingly sweet caress. When it ended, he whispered unevenly, "You're my girl, Smokey. Always have been. If you think a couple hours of making love can erase years, you're dead wrong."

Horns blasted, the band played "Auld Lang Syne" and confetti swirled through the air as Dan kissed her again. This time with a hunger that met her own and left her clinging to him.

In front of her home, Dan gripped her wrist to slide her across the pickup seat to him. "Dan..." she protested, as he raised her knuckles to his lips, kissing each one.

"Every time you say my name like that, breathless and low, I start heating up." He turned her hand, running his tongue over her palm. He sucked her fingertips, one by one. "Ask me in."

"No." Hannah tried to draw away, only to have Dan gather her closer.

"Too much has passed between us to back up, Smokey. Invite me in," he ordered in a deep rasp that slid along her body, and something within her began melting.

"You won't get me to sign over Ferguson land by spending a few hours in bed, Dan," she said unevenly, as he placed her hand on his chest.

"No? Maybe I was just thinking that there's no one else I'd rather be with on New Year's Day." Dan smoothed a tendril away from her forehead, lifting her hair in his fingers and studying the silky web in the moonlight. "I'll cook breakfast."

His body was warm and tantalizing beneath his shirt, a pearl snap opening beneath the light pressure of her hand. Big Al bellowed from the fence and Dan scowled at him. "Damn. He does that every time I'm here. He likes to head off for Black Arrow Arroyo about this time of year. Better watch him."

Hannah eased away from Dan and slid out the door. "I will. Thank you for the ride home, Dan."

"Are you finding what you need? Are you happy, Hannah?" he asked suddenly, his face in the shadows of the cab. The urgent tone in his voice caught her.

"Yes, I'm happy," she said quietly, then closed the door. They stared at each other through the steamy window for a long moment, before she turned to enter the house.

Seven

―――

January squeezed the valley in a cold, white fist, frequently breaking the electric and telephone lines and packing snow against the walls of the house. Despite the below-zero temperatures, the Ferguson homestead cabin stayed snug. The cattle milled around the pasture near the house and stayed in the loafing shed during the worst weather. Hannah devised a system of watering the cattle by hosing water from the house into small barrels loaded on an old sled. Apache pulled the sled to the water trough, where Hannah dipped and poured water for the cattle and buffalo. Galahad frolicked in the snow, standing a safe distance back from the livestock and yipping wildly.

Big Al followed her around the pasture and snorted when she entered the barn or house. Macedonia reluctantly left his stall to exercise.

Each day Hannah's pickup pushed through the snow-covered lane to the highway, then drove carefully into Jasmine. She worked on her presentation for redecorating Fallcreek Bank and fought dreams of Dan.

Doug viewed her sketches, okaying her swatches for drapes and carpeting samples. He was thrilled with the lobby sketch, instantly approving the mural depicting the history and settler families of the area. Hannah hired a woman, her husband and son to hang wallpaper, and they began on the conference room immediately. A professional muralist began laying out designs for the wall and a furniture refinisher began the process of stripping and restoring Doug's massive desk to its original antique cherrywood. Fallcreek Bank was to have a come-visit-awhile look with comfortable seating arrangements; the lobby would be last to be completed.

The Fallcreek account led to Doc Bennett's clinic and a rash of smaller businesses, as her schedule permitted.

Hannah worked with desperate determination, helping Isabel hang wallpaper and stain paneling. Completing her chores before daylight, Hannah coached the pickup through the snow to the road. Long after dark, she slid the pickup into the barn where Galahad waited amid the puppy wreckage of the day.

Then there were cattle to water and the warm sanctuary of the cabin and the luxury of her long soaking baths.

Through it all, Hannah admitted that she had never been happier.

Except for the aching need to hold Dan.

One night the buffalo circled the pasture restlessly, Big Al blowing steam into the frosty air. When she awoke the next morning, the buffalo were gone, having crashed through an entire section of fence.

An hour before dawn, Dan pulled up his collar against the bitter wind and backed Durango out of his pickup. Weather forecasters predicted a winter storm to arrive in full force the next evening.

"Hell of a time for Big Al to run for the Black Arrow Arroyo," Dan muttered, checking his saddle's cinches. "Doug shouldn't have waited until late last night to call." Hannah was missing, and when Dan drove through the snow-covered roads to her house he found it empty. Her pickup stood in the barn and Apache's stall was empty, his saddle and bridle gone.

After watering and feeding the stock, Dan had used a flashlight to search the outbuildings. One swing of the bright beam across the pasture told the story. Big Al had taken his herd to the Black Arrow Arroyo; after a make-shift fence repair, Hannah had gone after him on Apache. "Hell!" he'd exclaimed, fear snaking around his chest and tightening painfully.

"Hell!" he repeated when the flashlight's beam had picked up Apache's hoofprints covering those of the buffalo. He returned to the kitchen and scribbled a note, his hands shaking. "Call Else when you get back. I'm hunting you. Stay put."

Dan had taken Galahad to his house and made the necessary calls. A Blaylock male would take care of the puppy and tend the stock. If Dan didn't return within two days, Mike would begin a helicopter search party. Working quickly, Dan laid out his camping supplies with extra winter clothing for Hannah. At last, he made coffee and filled a big thermos, then a smaller one with hot soup, packing sacks with grain for the horses.

Every minute, fear snaked through him.

Big Al's instincts had drawn him to the ancient arroyo trail, taking a path sheltered by trees and brush. Durango followed the trail at a steady pace, and Dan strained for a glimpse of Hannah.

Damning Hannah's pride and the will that put her back against the wall, Dan adjusted his ski mask. He glanced at the dark skies. The weather front promised record-breaking snowfall within hours. In those few hours, he had to get Hannah to safety.

Dan slid from the saddle to check the buffalo sign, then swung up into the saddle. The arroyo was twenty-five miles away; Big Al and his herd had traveled the distance before in winter, returning when the weather changed.

Lowering his face into the warmth of his buttoned-up collar, Dan fought the wild fear washing over him.

"This could just cost her life," Dan muttered, filled with fear. He hadn't been this frightened since he'd pulled teenage Hannah out of that car wreck, raw pain curling through his stomach. If Apache slipped and fell on her... If the buffalo stampeded, catching her in their midst... If... If...

The cold penetrated Dan's thermal underwear, jeans and coveralls and he sipped the hot coffee gratefully, then urged Durango to a faster pace.

Dan's taunts sliced through him. His need for revenge had sent her into the sprawling snow-covered fields and could cause her death.

Rabbit and deer tracks crossed the buffalo tracks as the eerie, bluish white expanse stretched before him. The herd moved slowly, breaking the snow trail, the hoof marks not as sharply defined as when they ran. A calf trailed after its mother here; a big female had slipped and scrambled for footing across a rocky stretch. A small fir tree had been trampled, the core of the broken trunk slick with ice that had fallen during the night.

"Hannah." He'd taunted her, challenged her ability to survive.

Then twelve miles from the ranch, just as the early night began to shadow the snow, he saw the herd—big, looming shadows, foraging for food and drinking from an icy stream. Apache stood in the shadowy trees and smoke curled from a blazing fire into the darkening skies.

Dan's heart stopped beating, his heels nudging Durango into a faster pace. Apache whinnied and Big Al, a shaggy mountain of shadow in the blue-gray light, stood apart from the herd and snorted loudly.

Then Hannah was running toward him, stumbling on a fallen limb, the hood of her red down coat drawn tightly around her face. "Dan!"

Fear scraped away any of Hannah's expressions that he remembered, raking at him. His heart shattered with the terror riding him. *She was alive!*

He slid from the saddle, taking a few steps to her and swung her into his arms. She was trembling, her tears freezing on her lashes as Dan tucked her face into the warmth of his collar. "Oh, Dan, I was so afraid. We were coming back. I reached them a few miles back. But I got so cold.... So cold. Apache stepped in a deep hole, covered by snow. Two calves—"

She held him as though he was a necessary part of her. "There was nothing I could do," she sobbed. "They lay there trampled. Blood on the snow...and oh, Dan...their eyes, their eyes watching me, asking for help... There was nothing...I...could do," she repeated in gasps. "I built a fire to keep them warm, their mothers lay down beside them and let me share their heat...."

She began tugging him toward the fire and Dan saw the maimed calves. He drew his rifle from its sheath. "Honey, they're done for. All we can do is make it easy for them."

Staring at the calves, Hannah turned around, her shoulders shaking with her sobs. The buffalo started milling after the rifle shots, blowing steam into the chilling air. Ice clung to their nostrils and beards.

"Hannah, honey..." he managed, shaking with emotion. "We've got to go. If that blizzard hits when we're out here..."

"I know," she whispered, wrapping her arms around his back. "You shouldn't have come."

Dan gripped her tightly, only death could have stopped him. Then his spirit would have found her and guided her home. "You should have called me." But she hadn't, and a deep pain went ripping through him.

Hannah stood free, her face pale against the red hood of her down jacket. She brushed a thick woolen mitten across her face and sniffed. "I can manage...."

"Stop, Hannah... Tears freeze to your lashes," Dan ordered roughly and wondered when he'd begun to love her more than life. She didn't call him because he'd taunted her about surviving on Ferguson land for a year. He dabbed his handkerchief across her lashes and eased her chilled face into the warmth of his throat again. "You stay put," he ordered roughly. "A case of frostbite is the last thing you need."

"Stop telling me what to do, Dan," she muttered from his collar. "I'm glad you came."

He smiled grimly above her head. However frightened Hannah was now, she wasn't meek and she would survive. Only a special woman would care for buffalo calves, lying with them. Dan held her tighter, and her lips moved against his throat. "Stop shaking. You're the size of a bear. It's like an earthquake in here."

"When it comes to you, I can't seem to stop anything," he admitted roughly, delving into his saddlebags. "Step closer to the fire and change into these dry clothes." Stripping his gloves off, Dan spread his yellow storm slicker over the snow and eased Hannah down to sit on it. Working together, they eased her boots off and changed her damp coveralls and jeans for dry ones. When Hannah stood, Dan bent to tug on her boots. He lifted her onto Durango's saddle and poured hot coffee from the thermos, helping her drink when her hands shook too badly.

Apache nudged Dan, reminding him of the grain sacks. Feeding the horses, Dan glanced up at Hannah to find her watching him.

Watching him with her soul in her eyes...as though she'd be with him, a part of him through eternity.

The eerie half-light created by the white expanse caught her face. Her eyes were two large shadows in the blur of her face, her cheekbones stark in the pale, taut skin. Hannah's mouth looked like a frozen dark red rosebud. "I'm so cold, Dan," she whispered, a shred of terror echoing in the winter wind. "Cold in my bones. I couldn't go any farther."

There would be time later to scold Hannah. *If they made her cabin before the storm hit.* The damp mist was freezing on his skin now, circling them ominously.

"We have to make it back, Hannah," he said quietly, walking to Apache and tying his reins to Durango's saddle. Reaching inside his pack, Dan poured the hot soup and ordered, "Drink that."

When she obeyed, he arranged a thick down blanket around her legs and over her head, tucking it beneath her chin. "There, little one. Hold tight while I mount behind you."

Hannah's muffled whisper escaped the heavy folds. "I can ride alone, Dan."

He gripped her boot, terrified that the storm would hit before they reached safety. Nothing could keep him from holding her in his arms now. "Stay put, Smokey. I'm not in a mood to argue."

He waited just that fraction of time, poised for the hot slash of her tongue. "Are we going or not, Blaylock?" she asked simply.

He swung up behind her, circling his arm around her. Beneath the down comforter, Hannah's slender body leaned against him slightly as though she needed to melt into his bones. "Hannah...I..." He wanted to tell her of the emotion filling him, the shattering terror and the ecstatic delight that she lived. That she needed him. He gathered her tightly, tucking the fold of the blanket over her head. Then Dan began following the trail home. Big Al snorted, a haze of warm steam rising above the buffalo herd as they followed Hannah.

In the next hours, Dan struggled to stay awake, knowing that falling into the fluffy snowdrifts could mean death for Hannah and himself.

To rest Durango and to keep himself awake, Dan slid from the horse. He drew a flashlight from the saddlebag and began leading Durango.

Hannah moaned softly within the folds once, and Dan's heart stopped beating. He forced her awake, sharing the warm coffee and soup with her before tucking her into the warmth of the blanket. Once she struggled out of the folds, peering up at him in the night with huge eyes. "Dan, I..." Her lips trembled and she caressed his cheek covered by his ski mask. Then in a quick movement, she found the slit of the mask covering his mouth, kissing him hard. "Thanks."

The blizzard struck when they were three miles away from Hannah's cabin. As if sensing safety, Big Al and his herd began milling and snorting behind them.

Dan tensed and cursed, reining the horses away from the path of the buffalo. Hannah sat up, wrapping her arms around Dan. "What's happening?"

He ripped the ski mask away, working with the nervous horses to maneuver them back toward a stand of pines. Apache reared, his hooves striking the air wildly. Durango sidestepped, held by Dan's strong hands. "Hold on," he ordered Hannah grimly as Big Al snorted and the herd stampeded past them, heading for their feedlot in the pasture.

Dan cursed sharply, working to calm the horses and hold Hannah. When she gripped the saddle horn securely, he slid to the ground and cursed until the proverbial "sky turned blue." "That piece of stringy wolf bait has decided to come home for breakfast! Maybe he should end up in Jasmine's barbecue pot."

Hannah stood in the snow beside him, laughing as Dan glared at the thundering herd, retracing their path to the Ferguson feedlot. He blew a layer of thick snowflakes from his lashes, and braced his hands on his hips. "Women! What's so funny? That damn buffalo could have cost you your life!"

She grinned up at him, raising on tiptoe to kiss him quickly. "But he didn't. You came out of the night to rescue me."

He stared blankly at her wide grin and blinked. "Lady, we're in the middle of a blizzard with three miles to go and you decide the situation is funny."

"You look so frustrated, Dan. We'll make better time if I ride Apache," she said huskily. Something hovered and clung between them, the veil of thick snowflakes surrounding them as Durango shifted suddenly.

Against Dan's lips, Hannah whispered. "I wanted you to come, Dan. I knew you would."

Dan's kiss was rough and possessive, tender and hungry. "You belong to me, Hannah," he managed, the words tearing from his heart.

"Yes." The whispered word jarred him, made him weak and gave him strength.

He lifted Hannah to Apache's saddle, tucking her within the protective blanket. "You call me before you fall off, Miss Hannah," he ordered roughly, swinging up on Durango.

"Yes, sir."

Dan smiled grimly. If the storm worsened, Hannah's cockiness might give her the edge on living.

In the next three hours, Dan pushed hard for the house, taking Apache's reins. He kept a close watch on Hannah, running his hand down her back to let her know that he was there. Each time he touched her, she straightened as if he had given her strength.

When she didn't straighten, Dan raised his voice above the wind. "Did I ever tell you that you're a hell of a woman?"

Beneath the folds, her head nodded slowly and her back began to straighten. "You're full of bull," she returned pleasantly after a moment, her voice muffled. "Too tough for wolf bait and too mean to die...a throwback to your savage ancestors."

Beneath the ski mask, his smile startled him. "I suppose you're little miss sweetheart, huh? What about the time you sneaked the Wilson bull out to ride him and he bred every pedigree cow within two counties?"

"You'd just won good prize money at the rodeo in bull riding. I was going to show you up." Apache picked up his pace, nudged by Hannah's knees. "I'm going to show you up for a pansy, Dan," she called above the wind.

"That's my Miss Hannah," Dan stated with quiet pride. Then he saw the glow of the high pole light, dimmed by heavy snow. The fence had been repaired; Joe swung the gate open when they approached.

Else ran to them, fighting the wind. "It's a bad one, Dan," Joe called, moving beside the horses. Buried beneath the quilt, Hannah's body was hunched against the cold.

"Get her in the house, Dan," Else called, holding on to his leg. "Joe will take care of the horses."

Dan swung down, his body aching and stiff with cold. He reached Hannah just as Joe lifted his arms to her. "I'll take her," Dan said quietly, easing Hannah's hands from the saddle horn. When she protested, he said, "We're home, Hannah. Let me get you warm."

In the shadows, she turned sleepily to the sound of his voice. "Dan?"

"Yes, honey. Let me take you into the house where it's warm," he whispered soothingly, tugging on her glove. "Come on, sweetheart."

She grumbled sleepily, then slid into his arms. She wrapped her arms around his shoulders and clung to him fiercely.

In the warm house, he ignored Else's quiet offer to help. Placing Hannah on the couch, he stripped away everything but her lacy black bra and bikini briefs. "Dan, you look frozen to the bone. Get your things off," Else ordered quietly as she placed a soft blanket over Hannah. "The room is cool, keep it that way for a time," she said, tucking a soft cotton blanket around Hannah. "My, she's still our pretty little Hannah," she said gently, looking down at Hannah's pale face.

She smoothed a damp tendril across the pillow tenderly as Dan crouched in his shorts to chafe Hannah's feet. "Damn fool thing to do," he muttered, tucking her feet under his arms and rubbing her hands.

He blew on the slender, cold fingers, working quickly while Else stood back and watched. "She's a rancher meeting an obligation to her livestock. We knew Big Al would run back for a handout...Hannah didn't. She did what she thought was best."

"She needs a paddling until she can't sit on that pretty little bottom, that's what she needs," he muttered, tenderly chafing Hannah's bare arms.

"I'd say she's a match for my baby brother. A fine match for your headstrong ways. Is she all right?"

Dan ran his hands through his hair, then scooped Hannah into his arms and sat holding her as he wrapped the blanket tighter around her. "No."

Else skimmed Dan's taut, lined face and the possessive, tender way he held Hannah, as though no one could take her from him. "Doc Bennett can't make it through tonight, Dan. We used the truck's blade to plow through her road, but that steep hill out of Jasmine may be blocked."

Else examined Hannah's fingers and toes with years of experience in Wyoming winters. "I think she just needs to sleep it off. Joe says we can stay, if you need help, but there's a three-day blizzard on the weather forecast. He should get back to take care of our stock. Want me to stay?"

"No." Dan gathered Hannah closer, tucking his chin over her head.

Else adjusted the afghan around his bare shoulders and tucked the end of the blanket around his feet. "You didn't have to go after her. Mike could have taken the helicopter out when it cleared—"

Dan glared up at her, his hair in rough peaks and his jaw covered with two days' growth of beard. "Don't you have something to do? Nancy's daughter is about to have a baby. Go hover over her."

Else grinned widely. "Jakie's boy is staying at your place, taking care of the stock. They won't know how to act with a civilized man.... I feel sorry for Hannah, leaving her alone with you. She'll be fine, Dan. Up to fighting with your orneriness in no time. There's stew in the slow-cooker and plenty of groceries to last out this storm. We'll be leaving now, or we can stay here and protect Hannah from you."

She drew on her heavy coat and looked down at him tenderly. "She's where she belongs, Dan," Else said softly, patting his bare shoulder. "You keep her that way. I guess we'll leave you with her. But you call me as soon as she wakes up."

Holding Hannah closer, Dan looked up at her. "Thanks."

"You bet. I've been waiting to see this for years... Hannah and you, each needing the other. Call me." She bent to kiss his stubble-covered jaw and then was gone.

Dan sat holding Hannah for an hour as she slept, content to have her safe in his arms. Periodically he kneaded her toes and feet, working his way to her thighs, then repeating the massage on her hands and arms. She murmured, wakening slightly to look up at him. The drowsy, soft stare traced his face, her hand reaching up to stroke his hair. She urged him to her soft kiss, then fell asleep, snuggling back against him.

He held her for another hour, letting the fierce fear drain out of him, then eased her onto the couch. After stoking the wood fire, he crouched by her to take her hand and brush the soft skin across his lips. Exhausted, Hannah breathed deeply and would sleep for hours.

Dan folded his tall length into Hannah's tub. He bathed quickly, welcoming the heat sliding into his bones. Wrapping a towel around his waist, he ate and turned off the slow-cooker. In Hannah's bedroom he discovered an antique four-poster with flannel sheets and mounds of beautiful hand-stitched quilts. Using an electric heater, Dan quickly warmed the room and used hot bricks covered with towels to heat the bed.

Hannah protested the move to the bed, but Dan had to have her in his arms before he could sleep.

He dozed for an eternity, rousing to gather Hannah closer. She held him in a soft tangle of arms and legs, her cheek resting on his shoulder and her slow breath sweeping across his skin. Dan's last thought before sinking into the velvety deep sleep was that he wanted Hannah in his life and arms forever.

Then he awoke suddenly, fear snaking through him. Hannah was gone.

Throwing aside the heavy blankets, he leaped out of bed. "Hannah!"

Striding into the living room, he threw open the door to the other bedroom stacked with furniture and boxes. The bathroom, filled with steam and her scent, was empty. "Hannah!"

He found her in the kitchen, dressed in a long, tattered chenille robe, a towel wrapped around her damp hair. Hannah stirred the pot of simmering stew, looking quickly away from Dan's naked body. "Try not to bellow in my house, Blaylock," she ordered calmly.

Dan ran his hand through his hair and across his chest, trying to still the panic still clutching at him, his heart pounding with it. Galahad yipped and Gertrude crouched at her milk bowl, watching him with unblinking yellow eyes. Snow drifted against the window's plastic coverings, the scant daylight skimming into the room. "What time is it?"

"About four. I just finished feeding and watering the stock. Want some stew? Coffee?" Hannah's soft, husky voice barely reached him. Dan blinked, caught by Hannah's sensual beauty. The robe's missing buttons exposed a soft slope of breast and an enticing length of inner thigh. Desire slammed into him before he fully recovered from the fear and sleep.

"Taking care of the stock. You should have left that for me," he grumbled warily.

"My stock, Dan. My responsibility."

Dan wanted to argue with her, and at the same time love her right on the braided kitchen rug. Taunting him, Hannah's black lacy bra and briefs hung from a hanger attached to the old ladder. The kitchen scents washed over him—stew and coffee, then the subtler arousing scents of Hannah's bath and shampoo.

Dan swallowed, caught by his stark desire to sweep Hannah back into bed and make love to her. Hannah glanced at him, her gaze slowly stroking down his body to the bold, jutting evidence of his passion. Color rose from the tan collar of the worn robe, rising up her throat to her cheeks as her eyes rose slowly to his taut face.

Neither spoke, emotions swirling through the small space, enfolding them in a sensuous, breathtaking moment. Dan closed the distance in three steps and Hannah's eyes widened, the wooden spoon in her hand stopped.

When he leaned close to her and turned off the stove, Hannah didn't move. A vein throbbed in her throat, her lips parting as she stared up at him helplessly. Dan removed the damp towel, combing her hair with his fingers and savoring the feminine scents washing over him.

She was all he ever wanted. Slowing the spring thaw would be easier than stopping his need of her. He'd seen her like this in his dreams—big smoke-colored eyes filled with his reflection and soft with her emotions, her expression a blend of uncertainty and desire.

"Dan...I don't think..." Her voice caught, her bottom lip trembling.

"Don't think, honey...just feel," Dan whispered, bending to kiss that intriguing vein covered by silky, sweet-scented skin. Hannah's fingers clutched his forearm, paused, then slid slowly up to knead his muscled shoulder.

In three flicks he unbuttoned the robe, his hot gaze sweeping down the shadowy curves beneath. Hannah's fingers fluttered lightly across his chest, her lids lowering slowly as he reached to stroke her breast.

The soft curve filled his hand, the tender nub nudging his callused palm as Hannah's breath caught. He followed the shape of her breasts with both hands, watching her as he gently lifted and caressed them.

Hannah trembled, her cheeks coloring. He absorbed the heat and desire in her, the hesitant, shy way her fingers clutched, then fluttered over his chest and shoulders. She arched suddenly and gasped when his thumb ran across her nipple.

Dan slid one hand lower, stroking the soft expanse of her stomach with his palm. Though Hannah hadn't moved, her heat reached out to him, snaring him.

When his touch entered her, Hannah shuddered, her eyes closing. Dan found the soft curve of her throat, his face hot against her warm skin. Hannah cried out softly, her hand brushing him intimately before she jerked it back.

Taking his time, Dan trailed his kisses across her hot cheek and to her eyelids. Tension ran through her like an electric wire, he could feel it shimmering beneath his touch. "What's wrong?" he asked against her temple.

"Dan...I'm...not used to naked men in my kitchen...." she breathed before he kissed her softly, nibbling on the delicious corners of her mouth.

"Man," he corrected gently, sliding his other hand beneath the robe to smooth the delicate curve of her lower back and lightly explore the mysterious separation of her hips, cupping them. "Me."

She shivered, arching toward him. The movement thrust Dan intimately against her and she whimpered softly.

She glanced down at him quickly, curiously, then jerked her eyes back up to his face. Uncertainty, shyness and hunger blended in her soft dark gray eyes. "It's daylight and in the kitchen, Dan," she whispered huskily. She glanced down again, longer this time and shivered.

Dan eased back, his dark hands almost spanning her pale waist. "Are you frightened of me, honey?" he asked, fighting his desire to give her the time she needed. Because this time he intended to make love to her, wiping out Jordan and the quick, heated coupling they shared before.

She swallowed, a damp russet strand curling across the movement of her throat. "Not a chance."

Stroking the hair back from her temples, Dan circled the indentation of her navel with his thumbs. "Take your time, honey. Do anything, but just let me touch you.... Touch me," he whispered against her fragrant skin. He knew then that the scent of Hannah's body, shimmering beneath his touch, would slide into eternity with him.

Fluttering restlessly on his back, her fingers gently stroked the shape of the muscles beneath his skin, discovering him. At each new touch, Dan forced himself to wait. Then, when her hands skimmed across his chest, toying with his nipples, Dan caught her wrists, speaking the thought that had been taunting him. "Honey, whatever happened between you and Jordan, you're still shy of me."

The smoky heat of her gray eyes burned into him, her color rising. "If you tell, Daniel Blaylock, I'll never forgive you. I'll hunt you down and tear tiny, but necessary pieces of skin off you. In comparison, your Apache ancestors will look like pussycats."

Dan couldn't stop his wide grin, nor the soaring joy of his discovery. Hannah's hand thrust at him and he caught her upper arms, shaking her gently once, causing the robe to part. Her uptilted breast, creamy soft skin, tipped in a bud of mauve, caught the bare light. He touched the tip with his fingertip and circled the perimeter slowly, pleased that however frustrated Hannah was with his discovery, she hadn't moved away.

She looked away from him, hiding her secrets, and he waited, needing to know. "Take your time, honey," he said gently, watching the proud lift of her head, the light flickering on the tips of her lashes.

After a long moment, she licked her lips, moistening them. "I didn't know how...how lovemaking should be, Dan. Then we... Then I knew." She turned slowly to him. "It should be sweet like spring rain and fiery as a storm."

Dan stroked her hair, waiting. Hannah's gaze ran across his bearded jaw and shoulders, the rumpled peaks of his hair, then slowly across the expanse of his chest. She frowned, stroking his nipple and smoothing the line of hair from his chest downward. Her touch paused at the layers of muscle covering his stomach. "I was married and barely knew anything," she whispered softly.

He closed his eyes, holding and savoring this new facet of Hannah. "Touch me, Hannah. Hold me in your hand."

When she hesitated, Dan gently urged her hand lower. His flesh leaped at her gentle, exploring touch, thrusting at her. She stroked him shyly, watching his tense expression, before her eyes swept to him. "I never knew."

"Take your time, honey," he urged again, forcing himself to remain still as her inquisitive gentle fingers enclosed him.

Eight

The light slid down Dan's beautiful body, sweeping over darkly tanned skin and black hair to the paler shades from his hips down his powerful legs.

She touched the healed scar where El Capitan had gored him, then traced the broad width of his shoulders. Her palms reached to smooth his taut back, the rugged power held in check as she explored him slowly, moving around him.

Dan's broad shoulders narrowed down to his smooth waist, the skin sleek and supple and dark with hours in the sun. His heat scorched her body, hard muscles tensing as she trailed her fingers over the hollows on the sides of his hips. She followed the muscles and cords down the back of his thigh to his knee and calf, then traced the same path on his other leg. Powerful and lean, Dan waited for her touch.

Standing in front of him, she raised on her toes to brush a kiss across his hard lips. Dan barely breathed, fire burning beneath his sooty lashes. She smoothed his bulky hair-roughened thighs with her palms and he jerked, breathing slow and hard. As if she'd touched his heart, the very essence that made him all-male and mysteriously enchanting.

She brushed back the rumpled hair crossing his forehead, traced the thick brows as he trembled beneath her fingertips. Hannah slipped the robe from her shoulders and Dan's dark, heated gaze slid down her body, tasting it, exploring every curve and shadow.

The stark desire in Dan's expression reached out to her, heating, melting every delicate feminine instinct and filling her with pride. The hair on his chest glistened in the half-light and she nuzzled the intriguing nipple as his fingers tightened on her waist.

Drawing her against him, Dan closed his eyes and trembled, the hard line of his mouth softening. "You keep playing around, lady," he said quietly. "And I'll want to do some exploring of my own."

His desire shifted suddenly against her, foraging for warmth. The feeling was exquisite, that gentle prodding seeking her, waiting....

Dan's large hands trembled and smoothed her back gently, and she knew that she could move away easily. "Yes," she whispered against his lips.

Then he was sweeping her up in his arms and carrying her back to bed. In the shadows, he placed her tenderly on the bed, arranging her hair across the rosebud pattern of the pillow. "Are you sure you want this now, Hannah?" he asked slowly, as if the words were dragged from his heart.

"No," she whispered, tugging at his wrist until he sat on the edge of the bed. "Not yet."

Dan's dark gaze flickered down the pale length of her body, his palm skimming her breasts and down the soft inner sides of her thighs. "You're all silky cream and sweet heat," he murmured softly, bending to kiss her breasts reverently, nipping at them gently. "Taste like honey and strawberries."

Hannah's body tensed, reacting to Dan's husky, deep voice, her skin sensitized to heat as his fingers traced her ribs, the thrust of her hipbones. Then he was stroking her inner thighs, always higher until his eyes met hers. Hannah wanted him then, with a violence that shook her soul. But she wanted more....

Easing to her knees beside him, she kissed his shoulder, loving the feel of his hair-covered chest against her breasts. Gently urging him to lie down, she began to explore him again. Fascinated by the rough sweep of his hand down her breast to her stomach, Hannah stroked his chest, following her hand across the hard-sheathed muscles. She bent to kiss the scar on his jaw, nibbling away the pain he must have known.

"God, you're beautiful," he exclaimed huskily, his hand caressing her hips.

Something went soaring through her, the need to make him remember her forever.

She touched him, sliding her fingers over him and lower, until he arched slightly off the bed. Wickedly she smoothed him again, and got the same reaction. Dan cursed, trembling with his desire. "I hope to hell this is leading where it should be," he stated roughly, as his thumb brushed her breast and the tiny muscles within her lower body contracted in silken delight. "Otherwise, I'll be crippled for life."

Smoothing, caressing, Hannah ran her fingertip across the tip of him and Dan shuddered, his hand gripping the flannel sheets. She spoke aloud before she knew her thoughts. "I ached for you, Dan, so empty without you in me."

"Come here," he ordered huskily, tugging her down on him. "Say that again."

Before she could whisper more, Dan's mouth opened on hers, his tongue playing with hers until she trembled. His hands ran over her, claiming her with rough tenderness until she sighed, her hips moving against him. Then he entered her slightly, withdrawing and leaving her shuddering.

Her fingers tightened on his arms. "Tell me what you want, Smokey. Tell me you want me in you...filling you.... Loving you," he demanded against her breast.

Every feminine instinct urged her to lock her body with his, finding the ultimate pleasure, but she withdrew, watching him with mysterious smoke-gray eyes. Her thighs quivered, aching...and yet she refused to come to his terms. Delighted with his taut reaction when her fingertip touched him, she smiled softly. She'd never played with Ethan, never wanted to, and now Dan's desire incited her senses into a heat wave. Loving Dan needed every bit of her concentration; she wanted to prolong the ecstasy of him, vulnerable and tempting beneath her touch. His heat reached out to burn her hand and Dan shuddered. He lifted one eyebrow, challenging her to tell him she wanted him, burning and hard within her, loving her.

Then, tossing back a heavy curl, Hannah murmured, "Take what you want, Dan."

In a heartbeat, Dan snagged her waist and drew her beneath him. His desire poised at her intimate, warm heat as he rested over her. His deep, loving kiss spoke of hunger, promised love in the future. He smoothed the arched line of her eyebrow, his eyes dark with passion. "You were always mine, Smokey. Always. Nothing has happened to change that."

"Yes," she said simply, then drew him closer, her hips arching up sharply.

Sheathed in her, Dan rested his head on the pillow. Beads of perspiration formed on his forehead as he lay still, waiting for an answer she did not want to give. "We're a part of each other, Smokey," he pressed. "Always were."

He taunted her with his fullness, pressing deeper and withdrawing, pressing into her heat until nothing else mattered. Then she moved, her voice shaking with emotion, whispering against his damp skin. "Always. There's only you, my love. Take what we both want."

They were flying, he thought dazedly, their bodies seeking an ultimate earth-shattering goal. Hannah flowed beneath him like hot satin, her scent filling him, urging him in a tangle of silken whispers and waiting desire. She began to circle him, squeezing with feminine muscles, her soft sighs and hungry mouth drove him on. Her teeth nipped his shoulder as she cried out; then he was poised on the brink of fire and ice, filling her.

She stroked his back later, still locked with him, and he kissed the warm flush of her cheek. When he moved to shift away, she held him, raising her hips and smiling drowsily. "Is that all there is?"

Her hand touched him, then, and Dan rolled to change positions, his body hardening again. Seated astride him, Hannah closed her eyes, her muscles contracting, pulling him into desire. Dan suckled one breast, then the other, biting gently at the nub until she cried out softly. "Don't... Please don't ever stop loving me."

Locking her to him, Dan filled her, kissing and nipping the sweet scent from her skin. Running his hand low on her body he explored her gently, intimately as he never had touched another woman. Hannah went taut, her eyes closing, her body contracting around him wildly. "Dan!" she cried out, as passion went ripping through them both.

Later she cuddled against him, stroking his shoulder. "I never knew it could be like that.... Earthshaking..."

Dan caressed the gentle sweep of her waist and hip, refusing to let her legs untangle from his. "With the right person, it's like rainbows and honey, fire hot. Like a fever, a hunger that's so sweet you ache from it."

"Yes," she said quietly, curling into him sleepily. "With you, that's how it is...."

He lay there quietly, caressing the smooth sweep of her back and studying the room that reflected Hannah's loving touch. He remembered that when they came in from the storm the overstuffed couch was laden with rumpled blankets, sheets and pillows. Magazines and catalogs were piled beside the couch, topped with a half-eaten bowl of popcorn.

This bedroom reflected a country charm, a collection of hand-stitched quilts, large enamel basin and pitcher with a blue rose design that sat on an oak dresser. A braided cotton rug, sewn from strips of rags, lay beside the bed. Lacy curtain panels covered the windows, edged by cotton curtains of huge dark gold roses. A straw basket filled with green eucalyptus and dried weeds sat near the oak dresser, accepting the scant light slipping through the window. Dan studied the warm blend of textures and colors and decided that Hannah's decorating abilities had melded castoffs into a beautiful, comfortable, warm room.

But she didn't sleep here. She slept on the couch. Why?

She stirred and smoothed the hard pad of his shoulder with her cheek. "Dan?"

"Just thinking, honey."

Her hand rested over his heart. "What about?"

He wanted to know everything, to ask every question that had clawed at him for years. Caution told him to move slowly, to take only as much as Hannah was willing to give.

"We're in the same fix as before...not prepared," he said slowly.

She smoothed his rumpled hair. "Shh. Don't worry.... Go to sleep."

Dan chewed on the thought for a moment, then turned her closer in his arms, luxuriously tangling his bare legs with her soft ones. Her toes lazily stroked his and her breath swept across his throat. "It's a physical thing I've just never had corrected. My problem... Don't worry," she whispered drowsily.

Dan lay still, savoring the scents and the feel of Hannah sleeping in his arms and decided that Hannah could keep that one secret...for now. She crowded against him, her breasts warm and soft against his side. He pulled her closer, wanting her to know how much he loved her.

Wanting to be a part of her again. Dan's lids closed slowly and he dozed, afraid that Hannah would leave him as he slept.

He awoke to find her gone, fear raking through him as it had earlier. "Hannah!" he yelled, his feet just missing Galahad as he stood. "Hannah!"

Galahad began barking sharply, following on Dan's heels as he charged into the bathroom, flinging open the door.

Hannah lay back in the tub, her hair piled on top of her head, surrounded by frothy bubbles. Steam swirled out of the small room and Dan stepped into it, closing the heat in. "You sleep a lot," she accused, grinning.

"You kept me awake. I'm not used to being crowded off the bed with elbows and knees," he returned pleasantly, crouching by the tub to admire the picture she created. Foamy bubbles swished around her shining, wet breasts and he glimpsed a dark crest beneath the water. His hand delved beneath the bubbles to the soft, sweet cradle of her thighs, rubbing her tenderly. Hannah's eyes darkened instantly and her breathing changed. She responded instantly to his touch and Dan's pride went soaring. Her lips parted as he stroked her intimately, her breasts shimmering in the water. "Want me to help?" he asked huskily.

Then she was standing, mounds of bubbles sliding down her shining skin, her eyes asking his. The look held and Dan's heart filled with love, with tenderness. She'd come to him shyly, exploring him as she hadn't another man. And now she wanted him again.

Dan lifted her, dripping, out of the tub, swishing a towel around her before he lifted her to encircle his waist with her legs. Barely reaching the bed, Dan fell backward with her following him every bit of the way. Their desire flamed again, rocking Hannah to her very soul.

Hours later Dan grumbled sleepily and padded to the stove to add wood. He returned to the bed, lifted the blankets and slid into her arms as naturally as though they'd been together for years.

She loved having his head rest on her breast, stroking his crisp hair as he slept. Dan wouldn't let her leave his side, exploring and delighting in her passionate response to him.

They fed and watered the stock late the next morning and Dan began a snowball fight that ended with Galahad bounding around them as they lay in a snowdrift and kissed. And kissed.

The snow continued to fall and Dan called Else as ordered. "I'm expecting something good to come of you being stuck out there with Hannah. Make sure I'm not disappointed, little brother."

The day and night stretched, alternating between lovemaking and sleeping. Dan awoke at five-thirty in the morning to the scent of Hannah and the beat of music and an instructor counting, "One...two...three...cross over. There now, stretch those buttocks, heel out... Hold it. That's right! Now the other side..." He forced open one lid, searching with his palm across the empty flannel sheet to find Hannah.

"Hannah!" he yelled, flipping back the blankets and a rolled pair of her black lace bikinis. He swung his feet to the braided rug, and the strap of her matching lace bra tangled around his ankles. He kicked it off, stalking to the door.

Lying on her back, her arms folded behind her head and knees bent, Hannah exercised to the tape cassette. Dressed in her thermal underwear and nothing else, she grinned in him and continued to lift her hips rhythmically. "Hold it.... Hold it...." the instruction ordered. "Tuck those buttocks in, tighten those muscles on the inner thighs.... Hold it.... Hold it...."

Dan leaned against the doorframe and crossed his arms across his bare chest. He returned her grin. "You've got to be kidding."

"I'm not used to being cooped up inside." Hannah turned according to the instructor's directions, rising to her hands and knees. "I got in the habit every morning and at night." She extended one long leg and tipped her head back, arching her back. "Go for it or turn to flab."

"Uh-huh. I thought we did go for it, yesterday and to-day," Dan returned, entranced by the shift of soft flesh across her backside.

"Nah!" Hannah lay down and lifted her legs as directed. "I've just started the warm-ups. Coffee and juice are made. Help yourself."

He ignored the offer, listening to the steady cadence of the tape and glancing around the room. "I thought women exercised with the television programs."

"I don't have a set.... Tapes and a radio are enough."

"Uh-huh." Dan glanced outside at the powder-dry snow and then to Hannah's flexing body. When she returned to the hands behind-her-head, knees-bent position, desire slammed into him. "I think," he said carefully as he padded toward her, watching Hannah's nipples thrust rhythmically against the thermal cloth, "that there are better uses for your energy."

Hannah's eyes widened and she blew a tendril from her cheek. "Dan, *you've* got to be kidding!"

"No, ma'am," he returned firmly, scooping her up in his arms and carrying her back to bed. Within minutes, he eased over Hannah's naked body and whispered rawly, "Show me that part about tightening those muscles again...."

When she did, Dan groaned and closed his eyes. Hannah frowned, caressing his bearded cheek. "Dan, am I hurting you?"

"Like heaven," he said when he caught his breath. Then he was taking her quickly, bringing them to a shuddering, exquisite release.

In the aftermath, she stroked Dan's taut shoulders and he shivered involuntarily. "I did hurt you," she whispered, kissing his damp forehead.

Dan's slow grin moved across her breast and he stroked her thigh, his hand trembling. "No, you didn't hurt me. Don't you know what it does to a man to be . . . exercised with?"

She was quiet, splaying her fingers through his hair. The word dropped quietly into the shadows around them. "No."

Dan propped up on one elbow, tracing the shape of her well-kissed mouth. He kissed her again, taking his time until she gazed up at him with that sultry, steamy I-want-more look. Whatever sex Jordan had had with Hannah, it hadn't opened up her feverish ecstasy and hunger. Hannah knew very little about the intimate, playful details of lovemaking. She'd saved that portion of her life for him and made the giving sweeter. "You make me feel . . . you fill me to the top," he whispered tenderly.

Experimentally she tightened around him and Dan inhaled sharply. Then Hannah giggled, the sound filling the room and Dan's heart. She repeated the movement, grinning up at him as his body reacted full force.

He returned the grin. "You think you're hot stuff right now, don't you?" Then Hannah giggled again and tugged him closer, and Dan forgot everything but the woman he had waited for, loving him.

They sat on the floor in front of the wood stove later, wrapped in blankets and the aftermath of their lovemaking. Scattered on the floor and across Hannah's lap were old albums and photographs. Dan held up the black-and-white photo of seven-year-old Hannah, dressed in her frilly Easter best and holding Earl's hand. Iris stood apart, her expression filled with love. John's arm circled her shoulders and he shared that same expression.

Hannah's slender fingertips smoothed the photograph, tears forming in her eyes. Dan drew her closer to his side, brushing kisses across her forehead and temple. "They all loved you, Hannah." He rocked her, folding her into his arms. "You were their joy. The will was Earl's way of getting you back where you belonged."

"They loved each other, all of them," she whispered unevenly.

"And they loved you, including Earl's invalid wife—in her way. Margaret saw you as a living part of Earl...and she loved you. Earl fought the relationship with Iris as she did. Margaret knew what was happening. So did John. Then you were coming, and back in those days, an unwed mother and her child bore a stigma for life."

"My father—John—and my mother always seemed so in love—"

"They were, honey. What happened is a part of life. John called me that night after you came home from my place. He knew you'd heard him and Earl talking about Iris and had learned the truth—"

He could feel her unraveling, the years tearing at her as she remembered, her bare shoulders and long back tense as he soothed her. She brushed away the tears and shook her head. "I couldn't cry. All those years, I forced myself not to and now all I seem to do is cry."

"It takes time, honey, when the pain is deep. Time to heal. You're back, and they'd like that."

Hannah snuggled in Dan's arms, holding him tightly, and the old photographs spilled to the braided rug. Dan rocked her, her silent tears trailing down his chest. He eased Hannah into his lap, cradling her until she sighed shakily. "You're back now and that's the important thing," he said, kissing her softly.

They fed and watered the stock together, fighting to keep the path cleared to the barn and feedlot. When Hannah stood still in the swirling snow, looking toward Black Arrow Arroyo, Dan tugged her against him. "Those calves were lost because of nature, Hannah. It happens. Earl lost several that way."

She let him hold her, sharing her grief. He had a part of her, Dan thought later as she slept curled into him in a tangle of arms and legs. Neither spoke of the buffalo run to the arroyo, nor of Earl's condition that Dan oversee her decisions concerning Ferguson land.

On the third day, as Hannah stepped from the bathroom into the living room, she heard the weather report from the kitchen radio and Dan's deep, hushed voice. "Then what happened? Uh-huh...I thought Rachelle wouldn't last. Mark likes more experienced women. He left Susan for Janna, remember.... No, I don't think so, Sergio has a baby with Deana and he's not about to tell her about that night with Donna.... Leona ran into the ditch that night, she was drunk because she'd just discovered Ward's child from Alex."

Leaning against the kitchen wall, Dan held the telephone in one hand and a dust mop rested in the crook of his other arm. He rummaged through the hair on his chest, a line between his brows as he listened intently to the caller. His well-worn jeans unbuttoned at the waist and his freshly washed shorts, socks and T-shirt hung drying from the ladder. "Uh-huh. Phillip was blackmailing Rachelle because she had an abortion. She didn't think the baby was Mark's—"

He glanced up suddenly, sensing Hannah. Before he turned aside, Dan's expression was definitely confused. "Ah...that's okay," he said curtly, a flush running across his cheekbones. "Just give them a little more grain. I'll call tomorrow to check on that...ah, tape that wildlife documentary for me. Make sure you get the end this time and not the advertisements." He hesitated, glancing at Hannah as she slid against him. "Ah, you remember our deal, don't you, Mindy? That's right. Just you and me, nobody else. Uh...make sure you don't tape over the old ones."

After hanging up the receiver, Dan shot a dark look down at Hannah, then kissed the tip of her nose. "Business."

"Uh-huh," she said, amused at his defensive look. "What's up?"

He moved away from her, pushing the dust mop into the living room. The opposite corner of the room from her required his extreme concentration, a red flush sweeping beneath his dark tan at the back of his neck. "Business... cattle...sheep...just business."

"Sure," she said, stripping the towel from her head and shaking loose her damp hair. Dan looked so stricken that she couldn't help teasing him. "The John-and-Marsha-type business. Dan, you're hooked on soap operas!"

He rounded on her like a Western gunslinger getting ready for a shoot-out. His knuckles went white as he gripped the dust mop. "You've got an imagination, Miss Hannah Smart Mouth."

"John," she cooed sweetly, mimicking the breathless tone. "Marsha," she sighed later, teasing him with a wide grin.

He glared at her through the shadows of the room and the fire from the stove hissed, finding a drop of water. Then, placing the broom against the wall, he took a step toward her, looking all dark, arrogant male. "You usually putter around in the bathroom after your bath," he accused.

"Changed my style." She grinned, leaping up on the couch and bouncing on it. "Big, tough Dan Blaylock is hooked on soaps...hooked on soaps... Whoops," she jumped onto the floor, backing a step as he stalked toward her.

"John . . . Marsha . . ." she ended in a sigh, as she recognized Dan's dark, sensual look.

He unzipped his jeans, stepping out of them fully aroused. "I'll show you, Miss Hannah," he threatened in a deep, quiet tone.

"Whoops!" she exclaimed as he bent to lift her to his shoulder and carry her into the bedroom. Galahad barked wildly as the door slammed behind Dan.

They made love in the barn's hayloft and on the kitchen floor, and neither could get enough. Time hung suspended as Hannah discovered Dan's need to hold her against him. As though he feared she would leave. . . .

Nine

They tumbled to the floor in a tangle of blankets, limbs and laughter. Galahad started growling and pulling a blanket with his teeth. Gertrude bounded to Hannah's hips, then leaped up to the bed where she curled into a ball.

Dan leaned over Hannah, smiling tenderly. She brushed back a strand of glossy hair from his forehead and he turned slightly to kiss her fingers. "When?" he asked softly, smoothing a russet web of hair away from her bare shoulder. He bent to kiss the creamy spot, then her lips. "When?" he repeated, tasting the corners of her lips with his tongue.

"What?" she managed in a sigh, nestling closer to the comfortable pad of his shoulder and kissing it.

"When are you moving in with me? This place doesn't have enough room for—" He tensed as she frowned.

"What are you saying, Dan?" she asked carefully, her instincts scrambling. Dan was doing exactly what she expected—pushing for more, deciding what he thought was right for the situation.

He breathed quietly, the muscles of his body contracting against her softness. "You're moving in with me," he stated, anger flickering in his eyes as he crushed the silky strands of her hair in his fingers.

"Just like that? A demand, in lieu of a question? You're pushing, Dan..." she began, foraging for thinking space that Dan did not permit.

"Am I?" The arrogant edge of his deep voice sliced through the tender aftermath of their loving. The hair spearing across his forehead fluttered as he blew out a deep breath. "I want you in my home, in my bed. I don't see any reason to wait for anything now."

He trembled, his muscles tightening around her possessively as he frowned down at her. "Tell me that you had this with Ethan, damn you," he demanded roughly. "Tell me that you turned to fire and silk in his bed...snuggled into his arms as if you were a part of him. Because that's what you are, Hannah. You're a part of me, the same way I am a part of you."

His heart pounded against her breasts, his black eyes raking her face from wildly tumbled hair to the soft, well-kissed curve of her lips. The scant light caught the sharp planes of his face, the fierce frown and jutting stubble-covered jaw. Beneath her fingertips, his muscles shifted under dark, warm skin, and the marks of her passion raised small ridges. "You can't go back, Hannah," he stated arrogantly, breathing hard.

"Dan...I..." She wanted the loving moment back, smoothing the tension racing between them. She stroked his taut jaw, loving the rough scrape of his new beard against her palm. Not to be soothed, Dan tugged at her hair, arching her throat to his kiss.

"What am I to you, Hannah?" he whispered roughly against her skin, his hand skimming the length of her body.

"Friend..." she began, then stopped as his hand possessed her breast, caressing it in his palm. "I need time, Dan." She couldn't allow him to push her until she was ready.

"Playing games, Miss Hannah?" he demanded, running his thumb across the tender nub on her breast. "*Friend* doesn't describe our current relationship. Move in with me." He bent to draw her into his mouth, until she inhaled sharply.

Easing away, Hannah smoothed his chest. His heart beat heavily beneath her palm as though he were running a race. "I . . . no . . . I'm not."

His hard lips firmed, his long fingers gently shackling her wrist. "I don't know how you dance this fandango in Seattle, but here we get married. Maybe adopt a couple kids. If you want to work, here or away, I won't stand in your way. We'll work it out."

Dan was forcing her into corners she wasn't prepared to meet. "Just like that? Because you want to? I'm staying on Ferguson land alone. It's something I have to do," she whispered.

He cursed darkly and Galahad skulked into another room, his tail between his legs.

"Ferguson land," Dan exploded in a low roar. "If you think I'm going to hold you to that condition . . ."

"I expect you to," she returned. "I'll pay you back every cent you invested in keeping my land."

"The will can go to hell, so can the land. Earl wanted you back and so did I. . . . Maybe just to make your life hell for the time you dropped in. But the past couple days changed things. . . . Marry me or move in," he demanded again, spearing his fingers through the hair at her temples and framing her face for his tender kiss. "When?"

She answered the warm, questioning brush of his lips with her own. "I've got to prove that I can manage on my own, Dan."

He tensed. "All this—" His hand swept down her body, jerking her tightly against him. "—didn't mean anything to you, but a cozy way to spend three days of a blizzard? We could be spending every night like this."

"It meant everything," she returned unevenly, trying desperately to sort out her thoughts. Dan moved too quickly, sweeping from the dream of lovemaking and laughter to everyday living arrangements. *How could a moment so lovely be destroyed with a slash of a single word?*

"Life's short, Miss Hannah," he said flatly, shaking her slightly. "When something good comes along, you hold it with both fists. Or it gets away. I know that better than anyone.... Hell, I should have never let you leave...should have dragged you back here, married you and tied you up with enough kids to keep you from thinking about leaving." Then he rolled away, his arms behind his head as he stared at the ceiling.

She touched his shoulder, aching to tell him that she loved him, that she needed time to lay the past behind her, to make a new life with him. Then he turned to her, eyes burning beneath his lashes, his lips forming a hard line. "Fine. Have it your way. I won't ask again."

He was hurting, trembling with an ache that slammed into her. In the next moment, Dan surged to his feet, striding out of the bedroom. Hannah's first tear rolled down her cheek at the sounds of Dan dragging his washed and dried clothes from the ladder and dressing quickly. Galahad yipped excitedly; Dan muttered something about the crooked maze of a female mind, the door slammed and the house dropped into silence.

Trembling with emotion, Hannah lifted the blankets back to the bed she had shared with Dan. She closed her eyes, fighting the need to go after him. Dan nursed his own wounds, just as she did. To live with Dan before resolving her past would be unfair. To let Dan push her into marriage now could be devastating later. She wanted her life with Dan to be more than a living arrangement, meeting immediate needs.

Over dinner, she touched his hand on the table and he withdrew, slashing a grim stare at her. His anger swirled around them, heating her skin and dashing apart her carefully constructed plea for time.

Then he was lifting her into his arms, striding into the bedroom. He loved her desperately, repeating caresses that brought her to the ultimate glory. He loved her with a determination; she loved him just as deeply, asking for more.

In the morning, he dressed and leaned against the kitchen wall, looking big and tough and bitterly angry. "Tell you what, Miss Hannah," he said curtly, placing his cup on the table in a gesture of finality. He spread his legs and locked them at the knee, drawing on his coat, then worn leather gloves. "You want a no-strings arrangement, that's fine with me. If you want anything else, then you'll have to come for me. I'll come back for my pickup and Durango."

She stood slowly, head high to match his arrogance as she fought the tears clawing at her. "I came for you once, Dan. I won't again. Don't try pushing me, Blaylock."

"Maybe not. Get used to it. You're in for a lot more. Jordan may have given you a long rein, but I won't." He bent and kissed her swiftly, with a tender savagery that spoke of his possession.

Then he was gone, the door closing with a soft, deadly sound that ripped her heart apart and ignited her temper. She threw his cup at the door and it shattered into pieces, falling to the floor. Beyond the window, Dan leaned into the bitter winter wind, fighting his way through the snow to the main highway. Hannah placed her hand over her aching heart. Struggling in the white expanse, Dan looked so vulnerable and alone.

That night she lay on the couch, easing into the back and aching for Dan. Then the telephone rang and she leaped for it, clutching it tightly.

Dan's deep, raspy voice slid across the lines. "Good night, Smokey. Keep warm."

She closed her eyes, wishing he were with her. "Good night, Dan."

"Miss me?" he pushed softly, with a touch of endearing uncertainty, and she smiled.

"Maybe."

He chuckled, followed by the sound of a deep yawn. "You're in for big trouble, Smokey," he said before the line hummed in a dead tone.

February entered with bitter frozen temperatures and unending sleepless nights. On Valentine's Day morning, Dan

studied the pale stucco walls, the dark hardwood floors and
the yawning emptiness. After Hannah's warm country bedroom, his room was barren and cold. Neatly made, his bed
offered all the visual warmth of steel. The script he'd been
reviewing was tossed on the floor because he couldn't keep
his mind on it. A dresser, black with marred varnish, occupied one empty wall. Tacks pinned pictures of Hannah to a
board propped on the dresser.

His razor, shaving cream and after-shave occupied a small
portion of the bathroom shelves. Though the fixtures were
new and gleaming white and the room was heated, it offered all the warmth of a hospital operating room. Boxes of
native pottery, salvaged from attics and barns, and handwoven woolen blankets spilled over the shadows of a bedroom. His parents' old furniture and a collection of castoffs
filled the other rooms. One smaller room held an antique
swinging cradle. The downstairs rooms resembled..."an old
bachelor's house," Dan muttered, noting the absence of
plants, which flourished in Hannah's home.

He sank into his armchair, propped his boots up on a
scarred walnut table and surveyed his house. Except for his
computer, the entire house was filled with a collection of
make-do's. One room was piled high with cheaply priced
furniture he'd hauled home from auctions. Layered with
coats of varnish and scars, the massive old furniture belonged to the settler's era, a part of his heritage. There was
something timeless in the heavy, well-crafted furniture
sharing the room with his mother's treadle sewing machine
and enormous loom. The Fallcreek Bank held more warmth
than his house, Dan decided, glancing at a tumbling stack
of Indian baskets.

"The packrat of the Blaylocks," he muttered to the barren walls. The house seemed to shudder eerily around him
as though the rubble of his life had been stirred briefly.
Rising and padding to the kitchen, Dan dusted a crumb
from the massive old cookstove. He took a second look at
a smudge, then wiped away his fingerprints with a dish
towel, carefully replacing it over the oven's handle. Occasionally in the midnight hours Dan fried an egg for a mus-

tard-and-toast sandwich, splattering the white enamel. Or Else left a dish for him to heat in the warming oven. The stove stood like a tombstone, marking his solitary life.

He flipped through a magazine lying beneath a Spanish horse bit on his kitchen table. The pages rolled to a chrome-and-steel kitchen stuffed with buttons. He tossed the magazine aside and shoved his hands into his back pockets, looking out into the fields of snow toward the Camelot.

Every bit of extra money had gone to holding the Camelot and bringing Hannah back to where she belonged...with him. He'd watched the turns in her life through Earl, waiting. Now the distance of snow-covered miles and her will separated them.

He inhaled slowly, fighting back the emptiness curling around his heart. He'd waited years, and now Hannah held him off with an arm of steel. The Fallcreek Bank project was nearly finished, a grand opening planned in March. Hannah worked on Doc Bennett's offices when she could, helping the carpenters open up two small rooms into a large reception room. Her stock was well fed and she entered the town's activities as easily as if she'd never left. Hannah had helped with Portia Longman's wedding, adding quiet, tasteful touches that delighted the entire town.

Sitting next to Hannah during the wedding, Dan had found his fingers locked with hers. He forced his eyes to stay on the ceremony, but dreamed of Hannah wearing a white lace dress and veil, walking to him at the altar. Hannah had pulled her hand away, her head high when he glanced at her.

Dan studied the swirling flakes beyond the window and ran his palm across his stubble-covered jaw. Earl's will stood between them as surely as a wall of bricks.

A woman of pride, Hannah would fight to keep the Ferguson land. He admired her spirit, carving a home from the shambles of Earl's house and tending the cattle and buffalo that he had loved. The land caught people, snaring them to love it. Others fled from the bond and the hard work.

"Mule-headed woman," he muttered, realizing that Hannah deserved respect. Working against the odds for success, Hannah's expression was sheer delight and pride when she surveyed the cattle eating in the feedlot. Cattlemen born to the profession bore that same quiet pride.

Dan discovered the smile warming his face. Ripped from the security of Seattle, Hannah fought a painful past with a strength that few could match.

His eyes narrowed at deer sliding from the woods to eat from his winter feeder in the snow-covered meadow. Hannah needed tempting, and he'd waded right through the sweet aftermath of their loving with demands that he knew she could not accept.

A doe raised her head, listening, ready for flight, and Dan's heart skipped a beat. Hannah could run just as easily as the doe.

He placed his hand over the frosty patterns on the window. He'd pushed Hannah, realizing that her strength and pride needed time to salve the past and sort the future. She could decide to sell the property and head back to an easier life. He'd thrown marriage at her, desperate to keep her near him. Dan heard his back teeth grind.

The telephone rang, and when Dan answered, Else said, "Jasmine's Sweetheart Supper and Dance is tonight at the town hall. Hannah is taking a shift at the kissing booth. Time for flowers and dinner. Have you made a date with Hannah yet? Or can I tell Jake Tallman that she'd appreciate a call from him?"

Dan went still. "Jake Tallman. You'd send *him* after Hannah?"

"He's a widower and handsome as sin. Lovable, too. Not likely to end up an old bachelor. And I want Hannah to stay put this time. He just sold her his old tractor and plow. Delivered it right to her doorstep last Tuesday, when the roads were clear."

"Damn, you're mean."

"Goes with the territory."

When she laughed wickedly and hung up, Dan muttered, "Jake Tallman."

To provide money for the children's library, the Ladies' Literary Society contributed a hand-stitched quilt for the raffle before dinner and several money-making events throughout the afternoon. At three o'clock, Dan kicked the snow off his boots and hung his shearling coat on the racks beside Hannah's red coat. The smell of country cooking and roast turkey floated through the air, along with the latest gossip.

Beneath layers of red heart shapes and crepe paper, the kissing booth was open for business. Judy Freeman, a cute college girl working the booth, was relieved by Hannah and men of all ages lined up at the ticket table.

Hannah's pink sweater-knit dress clung to all the right places, her glossy lipstick matching the color of her dress. Dan closed his eyes, pulled out his pocketbook, bought out all the tickets and tried to decide which calf to sell.

She smiled when she saw him and Dan shucked that empty feeling dogging him since he'd seen her last. He plopped the roll of tickets on the counter. "Well?"

Hannah put every bit of her heart into the first kiss, hoping Dan would understand how much she missed him. How much she had to succeed at meeting the past. He tasted like hunger, excitement and slow, tender lovemaking. He tasted sweet and gentle and caring. When their lips parted, Dan stared down at her and flicked the string of tiny shimmering hearts at her ear. "Miss me, honey?"

"Maybe."

Around them, the crowd shouted, *"One!"*

He handed her another ticket and grinned lazily. "Make that two."

After five long, sweet kisses, Hannah forced her lids open to the crowd's shout. *"Five!"*

Dan ripped off another ticket and dropped it into the slot in the box decorated with hearts. "You're not using all those tickets here, Dan," she managed huskily.

He straightened slowly. "Why not?"

Reeling from his sweet, tender kisses, she tried to ignore the possessive edge to his tone. It didn't budge. "Gossip, for one thing. Two, it's expensive. I know that carrying the Camelot was expensive. I intend to pay you back."

His slow grin wasn't nice. "Doug Fallcreek has a big mouth.... My tickets are as good as anyone else's." He flicked the tiny hearts again. "If you don't want me using them here, step out from behind that booth and we'll step outside. I've designated myself as protector for the men of the county. Things haven't changed much since you were growing up and discovering just how much trouble you could stir up."

Taking a deep breath, Hannah gripped the counter. "When you want to be, you can be absolutely arrogant. I volunteered for the booth and later for the dance. You don't have enough tickets for both." She leveled a stare at him. "I'll try to leave the men in one piece."

He shrugged and the red ski sweater tightened across his broad shoulders. Leaning back and tilting his head to one side, Dan looked about as pliant as the Teton Mountains. "Smokey, from now on, I've got exclusive rights to those kisses. You start passing them around and things could get rough."

For a moment, Hannah envisioned a gunfighter laying down the rules to a trespasser.

"Don't toss that macho, possessive doo-doo at me. I can do what I want...." She spaced the words out, glaring up at him.

His eyebrows shot up, a dark beguiling grin spreading slowly over his face. "Doo-doo? Is that anything like plain old manure?" While she fought for an answer, Dan dropped the ticket in the box and asked, "Are you working or not?"

"Dan...." Then his lips moved on hers, slowly, seducing her gently.

"*Six!*"

"Back off," she whispered when she caught her breath.

He laughed wickedly and stroked her flushed cheek. "Not a chance, Smokey. You'll have to bribe me if you want me to move."

Bending down, he caressed her lips with his. "You save the good ones for me, honey," he ordered softly, nuzzling her ear and flicking the hearts with his tongue.

"*Seven!*"

She licked her lips, tasting him. "I'm not promising a thing, Daniel Josiah Blaylock. I'm not catering to your arrogance."

He lifted an eyebrow. "Then I'll make things tough for any takers. I recommend you step out from that booth."

"Blackmailer, snake, arrogant..." she began beneath her breath. "And I was so glad to see you, too."

Both thick black eyebrows lifted and something savage and male eased as though she had stroked it with her hand. "Really?" The edge of fire flickered beneath his heavy lashes, quickly veiled. He bent then and kissed her.

"Eight!"

"You're looking mighty pretty, Miss Hannah," he drawled, leaning closer. "Smell good, too."

The ninth kiss spoke of reverence and tenderness. "I'll save the tenth for when we're alone," he stated softly.

Later Hannah undressed for bed in a daze. Throughout the evening Dan had been the perfect, attentive gentleman, cramming his possessive tendencies away.

He'd won a sweetheart ring from the jeweler's contribution to the charity raffle and slipped it on her finger.

Lying on her bed, she lifted the ring to the light, studying the tiny diamond resting within a gold heart. Dan was up to something.

At the Bank's grand opening in March, Dan dressed in a dark blue suit, a light blue shirt and a conservatively striped maroon tie. His gaze moved down her cream suit and pale pink blouse appreciatively, brushing the length of her slim legs to her business pumps. When she flushed and lifted her hand nervously to pat her chignon in place, the sweetheart ring sparkled and Dan smiled that slow, soft, sensual way that caused her heart to beat faster. He ate a stuffed mushroom from the hors d'oeuvres tray slowly, dipping out the shrimp filling with his tongue. Coupled with the gleam in his eye, the erotic action reminded her of his devastating lovemaking. Unable to look away, Hannah's throat dried and her body temperature rose. "Miss me?" he asked after the rededication speech.

"Maybe," she returned, her legs unsteady as he moved closer.

Dan brushed back a russet tendril from the pearl stud in her ear. "You're working too hard, honey. Ease up. Have dinner with me over at Mamie's."

"Who's buying?" she asked, suddenly aware that his fingers had laced with hers, his hard palm flush against her smaller one.

"The gentleman always pays, honey," Dan returned easily, but his head tilted back.

"I'll pay for myself."

The scar shifted over Dan's hard cheek. "Not this time. Not when you're with me."

She tugged his tie, unruffled by his fierce frown. "Be Jasmine's trendsetter, Dan. Live a little. How are John and Marsha?"

He gnawed on that while she circled the townspeople pinpointing their family names on the mural. She turned suddenly to run into Dan's wide chest. "Okay," he said as though chewing around a steel spike. "This once."

A little while later, in the booth beside her, Dan leaned back and loosened his tie. He pushed away the remains of their dinner. "You're good, Smokey. Doug and Doc Bennett are pleased with your work. Comfortable, interesting, and businesslike. If you're so set on paying me back, what about decorating my house?"

The question hovered in the air while Dan scooped his boot beneath her pumps and lifted her feet into his lap. He ignored her resistance, slipped her shoes off and rubbed her insteps with his thumbs. Beneath the table, his large hands smoothed her calves. He lifted an eyebrow when she sighed luxuriously. "You could be getting this treatment every night."

"I do. Gertrude walks all over me." Hannah wiggled her toes and Dan's thighs hardened in response.

His hands slid higher, stroking the back of her thighs. "Still doing those exercises?" he asked huskily. His fingers caught on her garter-belt straps and he stilled.

Hannah's heart jumped into high gear, her throat drying. Holding her eyes, Dan traced the small rosebuds covering the snaps and ran his finger around the top of her nylons. His hand tightened on her thigh, a dark flush running beneath his weathered skin as he breathed heavily. "You're driving me crazy," he admitted between his teeth, staring hungrily at her mouth as she licked her dry lips.

His intensity frightened and sent her soaring happily. Hannah eased her legs from his and slipped on her pumps. "I'm not happy about the situation either," she managed.

Dan slipped his hand over her trembling one. "Ease up, Smokey. We can work this out." Then he said, "You didn't love Jordan."

Closing her eyes and searching for the truest answer, Hannah whispered slowly, "No."

"But he was good to you," Dan pressed, studying his water glass.

"Yes."

Dan ran his thumb over the condensation formed on the glass of ice water. The trail smeared the droplets until they ran into tiny rivulets. He breathed quietly as though finishing a fast race, then slipped his fingers through hers. "So?" he asked after a tense moment without looking at her. His finger slid across the tiny diamond on her right hand. "Do you want to see what you can do with my place?"

A week and a half later, Hannah eased Jessie down the snow-packed road to the Flying H ranch house. Galahad barked at the cattle in the feedlot as they passed, then turned to her happily. His tongue hung out and his tail wagged, threatening to topple Hannah's notepads to the floor. "Thank you for coming. I appreciate your support," she said to the puppy whose feet had grown into huge paws. Galahad moved as though his body, particularly his paws, were separated from his brain's directions.

As she approached, Dan walked from the barn toward the house. In a denim jacket, jeans and boots, he moved like a Westerner used to open spaces. He turned and waited for her to park the pickup.

Etched against the background of blinding snow fields, Dan was a part of the land and time gone by. Through the glass windshield, he seemed so alone, strong, yet vulnerable.

I need you.... I love you.

Hannah's gloves tightened on the steering wheel as Jessie caught a hidden, frozen rut and slid to one side. She found a safe stretch and eased down the road to park in front of his house.

"You need to weight the back end more," Dan said as he opened her door.

Galahad bounded across her lap and leaped into Dan's arms, licking his face happily. Hannah giggled at Dan's surprised expression, then his open delight. "That will teach you to start throwing orders at me."

For just a moment, Dan hovered between a hard retort and a grin. The grin won, disarming her completely. "That's the first dog that's liked me," he said, lowering the puppy to the snow. Galahad jumped up on his legs, begging to be played with, and Dan rolled him gently.

Hannah slid out of the pickup as Galahad decided that Dan could take the full onslaught of his antics. "Hey!" Dan exclaimed, delight in his voice as he crouched to rub Galahad's stomach. "What's this?"

"He missed you. He knocked me into a snow drift the other day, and he's banned from jumping on me. You're the next best thing."

Dan stood, brushing the snow from his legs. "Nice to know I'm needed." He slid the bag of measuring tools and notebooks from her shoulder and bent to kiss her.

The kiss lasted briefly, speaking of hunger and tenderness and need. "I'm glad you're here," he said quietly, easing a russet tendril away from her cheek.

"I'm anxious to get started, Dan," she returned, fighting the desire to hold him close.

The house ached for her touch, she decided, moving through the unfurnished rooms with Dan. When he opened the door to the room of antique furniture, she couldn't help running her hands across them. "Oh, Dan. They are beautiful pieces."

"Think so?" he asked, leaning against the doorframe as she examined a walnut buffet, then bent to lift a sheet from a large vanity and mirror.

"Beautiful. I didn't know you loved antiques." The pieces spoke of the people who had settled the land. A tall clothes closet stood against the wall, surrounded by four large wooden chairs with wide arms. Wooden chests of different sizes were filled with treasures, pewter mugs, Indian beads, an Apache woman's doeskin dress, handwoven blankets. A solid oak butcher block stood beneath a clutter of crockery and wooden cooking implements. Hannah ran her fingers along the scarred edges. "This was my mother's."

Dan's arms were sliding around her, tugging her gently back against him. "I saved what I could," he whispered into her hair. "Waiting for you to come back."

She rested her head against his chest. "I'm not going to cry," she promised, just as the first tear slid down her cheek.

"You cry when you want, honey." Dan kissed her temple and rocked her. "There are more things in the barn and another room. They're yours."

"Oh, Dan, I should have been here...." He turned her in his arms, sheltering her against the pain that came less often now.

"You're here now. Where you belong."

She rested in the comfort of his arms for a moment, inhaling the clean scent that was Dan's alone. "Better?" he asked when she stepped away. Just then she knew that nothing had changed. That Dan was still tending her bruises as he had when she was a child.

Smoothing the scar on his cheek, she lifted on tiptoe to kiss him. "You have your uses, Blaylock."

"So do you," he answered quietly, smoothing her hair gently. "You've made everything right again."

She looked up at him. Dan shared a past and shared more of her present than any other person. *I need you.... I love you.*

Galahad flopped on Dan's boots and the moment eased gently away. "He likes you," she whispered when Dan's expression changed to sheer frustration and he reluctantly released her.

He ran his hand across his jaw. "I don't get it. Little girls love me. Babies, too. Horses, cats, chickens...everything but dogs. Now this one," he nudged Galahad's sleeping body with his toe, "suddenly takes to me."

"Dan!" Hannah spotted a heavy piece of furniture behind two tall dressers, easing around them until she could touch the enormous, upright loom. "Dan, that's your mother's loom! Oh, I remember her sitting and weaving. She wove my doll a blanket. Let's put this in the window light in the front room.... I'll come back tomorrow and start right away."

Dan stood back. "You're the boss. Anything you want me to do?"

"Move the loom if you can. That will give more space to maneuver in here and the front room is perfect for it." Hannah surveyed the furniture, speaking quickly. "The chopping block to the kitchen, those four wood chairs to the living room—I'll need to measure them for cushions. That largest walnut chest to the living room and the clothes closet to the biggest bedroom.... Ah, put this woven rug under your mother's loom, the siennas, creams and blues are gorgeous."

She eased between two dressers. "Stripping furniture is expensive, Dan. It would be worth the money and effort. The wood will be fabulous under the varnish." She turned to him. "It's up to you."

"When do you want them?"

"You'll probably have to have a few pieces done at a time...."

"Uh-huh. They'll be ready next week."

"Next week? Dan, it takes time to strip and rub a nice finish into beautiful wood."

"Okay. They'll be done on Monday."

Hannah took a deep breath. "If you're making fun of me..."

"Honey, trust me," Dan answered easily. "Do you want me to clear out my collection of pottery and blankets—"

"Where?" Hannah demanded, stepping over a dry sink to walk out the door. "Show me."

"Damn, you're pushy," he said amiably, leading her down the hallway to another room.

Pottery and blankets in different shapes and sizes tumbled around the small room. "Dan," she breathed, clasping her hands together in a delight that consumed her. "Oh, Dan, I do so love you."

Ten

Sitting in his easy chair, Dan listened to Hannah's ideas for decorating. Excitement hummed through her like high-voltage electricity.

Amid a jumble of pottery, blankets, antiques and her notebooks, Hannah sat Indian-fashion on the floor. The late-afternoon light tangled in her hair, catching in the fiery tips. The measuring tape, tossed over one elegant shoulder, shifted as she moved. "The real basics are here, Dan. You could use some odds and ends, like area rugs and towels."

A professional working at her craft, Hannah focused on the project, allowing him to study her quietly. During their exploration of his house, Hannah moved constantly. A slender hand brushed softly across a soft merino wool blanket, tracing a peach-and-cream stripe. A loving finger-tip traced the lines of a chest, the lip of a tall pot washed in blues and grays.

An artist deep amid her trappings and thoughts, Hannah loved her craft and the challenge. She absorbed the colors and textures as though she were inhaling exotic perfumes, testing them with her mind. He'd missed this portion of her life, the professional woman at ease with a challenge and her skills. Dan savored the moment, wrapping it inside him, a facet of Hannah to explore alone in the night.

Framed against the darkening shadows, Hannah studied the area she had designated for the loom. She'd stripped off her socks and tapped the hardwood floor with slender toes tipped in blazing red.

The slow rhythm of that slender foot set his blood heating. Pale, delicate skin against dark wood . . . the colors of their bodies . . . His fingers latched to the armchair, anchoring him from her.

Hannah frowned, scribbling a note, and he followed the delicate line of her throat, the sunlight sliding down a tendril curling around her ear. "Cooking pots and pans, utensils. A dining table and chairs, but just the right ones . . . We'll work on that. They should match the other wonderful pieces. A bookcase stained in dark walnut could be built in that small room. . . ."

Hannah jerked a pencil from behind her ear and Dan wanted to taste the soft flesh. She pointed down the hallway. "It would make a wonderful office." Hannah glanced at him questioningly. "Unless you're more comfortable out here."

"Put me where you want me," Dan answered, thinking that if she put him anywhere within touching distance, he'd be pleased. At the moment he was thinking of her excitement earlier. . . . *Oh, Dan, I do so love you.*

He raked his hand through his hair. A few pieces of discarded furniture, some musty pots and blankets, and Hannah tossed him the words he'd wanted for years. Dan had forced his boots to remain in the hallway and strained against his body's need to cross the shadows to Hannah. He wanted her tangled in his arms, loving him with sweet kisses and hungry, soft noises.

Hannah tugged on her socks. "I'll bring my sewing machine over, if you don't mind the clutter. There is this gorgeous swatch of upholstery material that would be wonderful on those armchair cushions. The cream color can run across the room with a pad on that longest chest. It would be perfect for a window seat. And cream will open up the shadows.''

Hannah snapped her notebook closed and yawned, stretching her arms high in a movement that dried Dan's throat and hardened his body. "Move in what you want. What you need..." *Share my home.... Live with me.... Love me....* he finished silently as she began stuffing her measuring tapes and notes into the bag.

Fear snaked through Dan as Hannah uncurled and stood. In minutes she'd be leaving, taking her warmth away, and the house would echo with her scent.... He came to his feet, muscles tensed, searching desperately for a reason to hold her. Then she looked up at him and smiled. "I think you'll be really pleased with the moderate cost.... What's to eat? I'm a starved woman."

Dan blinked, trying to bridge his fear, the insight to her professionally and food. He'd remembered to hide his glasses and the board with her pictures; he'd cleaned and dusted for her visit... and hadn't thought of food. "I'll dig up something."

"Great." She pointed to his favorite chair. "That will have to go or be upholstered."

Dan stepped back, surveying the comfortable chair covered with a blanket. "What's wrong with it? I like it the way it is."

"Dan, it's ratty," Hannah stated gently, tugging aside the blanket covering the sagging cushion and worn fabric.

He replaced the cloth, smoothing it. "This stays put. I like old, sagging things... like you," he teased, unable to resist. "Are you still exercising?"

Hannah's cheeks began to flush and she bent to pick up her bag. "Blaylock, you are amazing," she said when she straightened. She thumped his chest with her fingers. "You make one wrong move, buster, and I'll saturate this place with ruffles and lace. I've got to get back to the Camelot."

"Why?" he demanded, trying to rein the need to hold her for eternity. To make her whisper those words again, only this time in his arms where he could see himself filling her dark gray eyes.

Then Hannah was stepping next to him, bringing his head down for her soft, lingering kiss. She stroked the back of his taut neck and the terror within him eased. "We'll play this fandango my way, Dan. Or not at all."

She kissed him hard, winding him. But before he could react, Hannah walked out the door.

"Women," he muttered to Galahad, who flopped across his boots and ignored Hannah's call.

On her way to the Flying H gate, Hannah passed a Blaylock caravan. Logan and his girls came first. The girls waved from the pickup, and Logan politely doffed his Western hat. Else and Joe with their teenage grandsons passed next, and the males in the cab nodded an acknowledgment. Rio and Roman Blaylock passed in a cattle truck on the narrow lane, then Jake Tallman followed. Each male tugged his hat politely, acknowledging her as a lady.

Five other pickup trucks in various sizes and colors passed her, filled with children and wives. Apparently the Blaylocks were having a family reunion.

Hannah looked in her rearview mirror and found herself smiling. Dan's delight with Galahad had prompted her to temporarily leave the puppy. But Dan's house needed a family to fill and warm it. The Blaylock tribe would do a good job of that tonight.

She carefully maneuvered across an icy patch on the road. Her house waited beyond the night, and Gertrude would be impatient for her milk.

I do so love you.... The words had flown out of her when she discovered his secret hoard of pottery and blankets. Dan had stood at the doorway, his big body tensed, his fists at his thighs. His expression was one of fierce longing and of love, of fear and disbelief.

She wanted him in his prime, when she said those words again. When they could both handle the moment, the chains of the past and the will behind them.

In the silvery wedge of her mirror, the woman's lips curved warmly. Hannah intended to give Dan a home that would reflect his love of history and the people who settled the land. Payments for the Camelot aside, she wanted to give him a special gift for his kindness to her uncle. She wanted to give him something of herself....

The next day, she fed and watered the stock with a lingering, last study of Macedonia. His eyes had taken a faraway, shadowy look, worrying her. The veterinarian had assured her that Macedonia's health was good for his age, his decline natural.

When Hannah arrived at Dan's at ten o'clock, she found a note taped to his front door. "Letterman's barn roof caved in last night. He lost stock. Helping out there."

Happy to see her, Galahad raced across the gleaming hardwood floors, sliding on the newly waxed surface. He dropped a pair of Dan's boxer shorts at her feet and grinned up at her, tongue hanging. "Wonderful," she said, rubbing his ears. "Dan does wear these well, doesn't he?"

The heavy furniture was gone and scents of cleaning solvents filled the house. The hardwood floors gleamed, newly waxed. The refrigerator was stocked and two folding picnic tables replaced Dan's desk arrangement.

The light from the window shot through the wool threaded on the loom, the large chest placed beneath the window. Her mother's kitchen block stood in the kitchen. "The Blaylock elves and fairies have been busy," Hannah murmured, easing her sewing machine on the table.

Elizabeth Blaylock's loom beckoned to her, memories floating around it like dust specks in a shaft of sunlight. Skeins of hand spun wool—cream, dark red, browns of rich earth colors—rested in a box, waiting for Hannah to finish their cycle.

Galahad scampered away, returning to drop Dan's dirty jeans at her feet. When she retrieved them, the puppy ran off again, dragging back more laundry.

"You're telling me to get busy caring for the man, right?" Hannah asked, gathering the clothes and seeking out Dan's washer. She worked efficiently, making more notes on the rooms. Taking a break at Dan's desk in the small room he had accepted for his office, Hannah decided to keep track of her expenses and notes on his computer.

After ordering upholstery material, she rummaged through the computer files, looking for an acceptable program. Dan's extensive notes on the Western theater were neat and she accessed an accounting file. The Flying H and the Camelot expense sheets blazed back at her from the screen. The Camelot had been eating the Flying H's income from the sale of cattle and grain for over ten years. Dan's financial accounting files laid out his economic picture clearly: his expenses ran to cattle and little for himself. His savings and checking accounts resembled a shaved pancake. In a bad year, he could lose the Flying H. Scanning a file marked "Sales," she trailed the efficient breeding and sale of his two hundred cattle. Hannah clicked off the computer and sat back against the chair, sipping her coffee.

"Dan was paying long before my uncle became ill," she murmured, noting his rodeo trophies and wall plaques. A check stub for several thousand dollars with a movie company's trademark marked a black ledger. She opened the ledger to scan Dan's extensive earnings as a movie consultant. Training horses and their riders, Dan turned a neat profit, which the Camelot quickly devoured.

"Oh, no," she whispered, remembering the upholstery, drapery materials and wall hangings she had ordered. Hannah covered her face with her hands and shuddered. Then, forcing her back straight, she stood and began walking around the house, rearranging her notes. "Daniel Blaylock, you are going to have a beautiful home. I am fighting you on my terms, without gratitude."

After canceling the order for the expensive fabrics, Hannah reordered a durable nubby cream material that would arrive the next day.

Hannah hung the striped soft merino-wool blankets on the outside clothesline with Dan's clothes. Keeping a running list of needs, she carefully sorted Dan's artifacts and selected Spanish trading beads and spurs, placing them aside with the box of skeins.

Logan was the first to arrive late that afternoon, carefully backing his truck to the porch. Roman Blaylock, a younger brother, helped move an upright chest and the old buffet into the house. Stripped and rubbed with oil, the wood gleamed richly. Logan grinned and nodded courteously. "Ma'am. Where do you want these?"

Rio Blaylock, the youngest brother, backed his pickup in later and the men carried an immense four-poster walnut bed up the stairs and assembled it in Dan's room. Rio smiled his female-slaying best and nodded. "Ma'am. Dan better be happy with this. I had to back out of a date with Lacey Morgan to work all night on this monstrosity. The fire at Wilson's cut into my time this morning. Dan left Letterman's to help out and he's still over there."

Logan stared at Rio. "Why is Else leaving you alone? She's thrown everyone else into the marriage arena."

"I'm her favorite. She wants to keep me," Rio answered easily, lifting Dan's mattress and springs onto the bed. The three tall men surveyed Hannah appreciatively.

"You'll do," Roman said quietly, nodding as he passed her.

Dan called her at the Ferguson house late that night. "Smokey?" His voice was rough, tired and threaded with uncertainty.

"Yes?" She placed her lists for fabrics and notions aside, concentrating on the sound of Dan's deep voice.

"You coming back tomorrow? Or are you letting me clean up this mess?" he asked.

"I'll be back," she answered, wishing she could hold him.

"Miss me?"

"Maybe."

He laughed softly then, the bedsprings creaking in the background. "What's this going to cost? Or should I ask?"

"You can afford it." Hannah closed her eyes, seeing Dan stretched out on the four-poster bed. She glanced at her blankets on the couch and hugged the dream of those precious days together. One day at a time, she promised herself, studying the woven wall hanging she had just begun.

"I like the bedroom. The way you stacked the baskets and big pottery vases and used those wool blankets. . . . Remember Smokey, you can back out at any time."

Dan turned the borrowed pickup off the state highway and his headlights speared the night, finding the lane to his house. The chase of the wild dogs had taken him across the mountains, and he ached in every muscle—the ones that weren't frozen through.

The pack cut a swath across the country, preferring isolated, helpless livestock. Hunger had brought them to Dan's herd. El Capitan's horns were red this morning, his hooves stamping the snow as Dan passed to feed the stock. In the half-light preceding dawn, a dead dog lay within yards of the young bull. Feeding his stock quickly, Dan tucked Galahad safely in the house and attached a scope to his tranquilizer gun. Mike agreed to pick up the animals for a shelter later. Adding a gun belt and pistol for safety, Dan had saddled Durango and followed the pack's trail into the pink dawn.

Strengthened by a fresh doe kill and hating man, the big pack had jumped him a half hour after Durango's nervous warnings. A mix of big dogs showing a strong wolf strain, the pack worked to try and hamstring Durango. While they moved easily on the crust of the snow, the heavily weighted horse struggled as Dan fired rapidly. There was no time for tranquilizers and Dan fought to survive.

In the next moment, the eight biggest dogs lay dead in the snow, the smaller members of the pack running away. Mike's helicopter hovered in the gray afternoon sky and Dan waved him off. Durango needed attention and Dan broke a trail through the snow to the Diegos' spread.

He eased the pickup over a stretch of ice and noted the smoke winding from his chimney, the light from the kitchen windows slashing against the cold night.

Tired and cold, Dan sighed. He desperately needed Hannah waiting for him and dreaded entering the shadowy echoes of the empty house. In the two days of rebuilding the barn and hunting, he was exhausted and a wakeful night without Hannah warming him waited. . . .

Hannah's pickup stood at the house and Dan parked beside it. His heart began an erratic beat, his mind working on a dream that could be shattered by a moment's reality. He entered the house quietly, slipping off his coat and down vest.

The scents of foods filled the warm house, trapping Dan. He listened to the sounds of Hannah humming in the kitchen—pans clattered and water ran in the sink.

Hannah! He edged toward the kitchen, avoiding the swath of cream material that tangled across the floors and crawled up to her sewing machine. He sidestepped a mountain of cushions amid the rubble of their old coverings, then stood in the shadows outside the kitchen door.

Her hair piled high in a tumble of dark red curls that trailed down her neck, Hannah stirred a pot on the stove. In jeans and his T-shirt, which fell flowing to her knees, she was everything he'd wanted for an eternity.

Tangled in his dreams and reality, Dan forced himself to breathe quietly.

Galahad surged around a corner and threw himself at Dan's legs in a flurry of welcoming yips. Hannah turned, the wooden spoon stilling in her hand. Her eyes widened, taking in his new beard and flowing down his dirty clothes and the gun belt strapped to his thigh. "Hi, Dan... Welcome home," she said softly, her eyes filling with him as he closed the distance between them. "Supper will be ready in just a minute.... Go wash up...."

Then he was pulling her hard against him, absorbing the soft shock of her body against his tired one, fighting the fear that this was the Hannah of his dreams....

In his arms, Hannah's warmth eased that fear. She clung to him, meeting his hungry kiss with her own. Trembling as her hands ran over him, smoothing his cheeks, Dan tasted the silky welcome of her lips. He ran his hands down her curved body, holding the dream and tracing warm, pliant flesh.

Were the tears hers or his? Were the years shattering apart and leaving him whole again?

Filled with the exotic scent clinging to her, Dan shuddered, forcing his mouth to lift from hers. He spanned her waist with his hands, fearing that the dream would evaporate.

Her arms locked around his neck, as though he were the missing part of her. Dan pulled her gently against him, burying his face in the warmth and scents of her throat.

A long moment passed as they held each other and then Hannah raised on tiptoe to kiss and nibble his ear. She tugged his belt lightly. "Tell you what, cowboy. You take off that gun belt, shower, eat supper, and we'll see what happens next."

He protested by drawing her closer, cupping her hips in his palms and lifting her against his aroused body. "We could see what happens now."

She lifted an eyebrow and kissed his lips lightly, following the contour from side to side in a sensuous caress. "I'm not going anywhere. Your brothers have taken care of your stock and mine. We've got all night."

Closing his eyes, Dan wavered between taking her suggestion and claiming her on the kitchen floor. Fearing that she would leave, he lifted her wrist to his lips. "Take that shower with me and it's a deal."

"The pot roast would burn. The gravy would turn lumpy and the shower stall is too small," she returned smugly, grinning.

Dan took the pencil tucked into her hair and tossed it aside. He mentally measured the shower and decided that he'd prove her wrong later. He was startled to find himself returning her grin, to laugh as she began to tug his shirt free. "I am a hungry woman, Blaylock. You're standing between me and my food, and that's dangerous," she teased, kissing him. "Move it, cowboy."

"Sassy woman." Dan reluctantly eased his hold, beginning to strip off his gun belt. The sound of something simmering caught him, turned him toward the stove.

He stood quietly, staring at the rolls warming in the oven, a browned roast circled by potatoes and carrots simmered in its juices, filling a dented pot. A dish towel served as a potholder for the cast-iron lid that had been set aside, and the makings of a salad were strewn across the counter. Wooden spoons stood in a bowl on the shelf over the burners with a variety of spices in old jars. Hannah's notebook lay open near a stack of new dishes, thick cream pottery circled by a sienna band.

Hannah's arm lifted to his shoulder, finding and kneading a tense cord. Wearing scents of exotic perfume, her bath and freshly baked bread, she leaned against him. "I love this stove, Dan. I hope you don't mind..."

Swallowing the dry wad in his throat and fighting the loss of his pride, Dan nodded curtly. "Stoves are meant for cooking."

She smoothed his shoulders with her palm, then slipped her arm around his waist comfortably. "Especially this one. It's marvelous."

Pushing his luck, he turned and looked down at her. Flushed from his kisses and leaning against him, Hannah had never been more beautiful. "You said you loved me," Dan managed, while fear rippled coldly up his spine. "Did you mean it?"

His heart waited, exploding with emotions; his lungs ached for air that he dared not breathe, fearing the dream would fly into the cold April night.

"I've always loved you, Dan," she admitted quietly, her gray eyes velvety soft and brimming with tears. "Too much for my own good."

Galahad began barking for attention, leaping on Dan's legs and begging to be included. After a moment of drowning in Hannah's soft eyes, reading emotions he'd dreamed about, Dan muttered, "That damn dog."

"He loves you, too," Hannah answered slowly, rising to kiss his jaw.

A fire woman coming after him, Dan thought when she carried their plates into the kitchen, then stood at the kitchen door.

In the living room he rose slowly, trying to read her face in the shadows.

The light caught her hair, framing her head in fire. Her heat snared him, the scent of her silky flesh slid to him. "Smokey?"

She took a step toward him, then found the snap of her jeans, shucking them aside.

Dan's throat dried, his hands trembling and his feet locked to the hardwood boards. The T-shirt revealed the long curved line of her legs, the strength and suppleness of a woman who enjoyed movement. Hannah lifted her arms, the soft cotton material flowing away from her until she stood dressed in a tiny strip of lace.

She stepped nearer and her hair cascaded over a bare shoulder. She kissed him hard as his hands dragged her against him.

Then Dan lifted her, carrying her up the stairs to his room. At the threshold, she'd gripped his hair hard, tugging his head down until their eyes met. Dark as smoke in the night, her eyes filled with tears. Just as the first tear hit his throat, she whispered unevenly, "This better be good, cowboy.... I was so frightened.... You go tearing off after danger again without me and I'll hunt you down."

He dropped to the bed, taking her with him, hunger burning fever hot as they came together. Poised on the brink of the first wave of passion, Dan fought release. With their fingers clasped tightly beside Hannah's tousled curls, passion speared through them at the same moment; in the next heartbeat another crest began.

Heat. Silk. Hunger. Dan fed on the flow of her body beneath him, over him. Meeting on the blinding summit, they fell gently, reluctantly into each other's arms. She clung to him drowsily, and he covered them with the tangled sheet and blankets. Then Hannah reached for him again. He loved her desperately, holding her as she fought to bring him closer, yielding a little as she locked him in her warmth.

Lying with Hannah in his arms later, Dan drew a cream sheet over her bare shoulders and pulled her closer. Too exhausted to sleep, he settled for reliving each moment of his homecoming and their hungry, tender lovemaking.

Her thigh settled comfortably within his, her cheek resting on his chest. She held him as though an eternity would pass and she'd still nestle at his side.

On the rug beside the bed, Galahad yelped softly in his sleep.

Hannah stroked Dan's chest, touched his waist and gathered him closer.

Before Dan dropped into sleep, he decided he'd taken a fire woman to bed, breathing her tantalizing scent and burning in her hunger. Smoky gray eyes promised fire, her hair blazing across her pale skin and binding him as surely as cord.

Before dawn, Hannah moved over him, flowing around him like hot silk, feeding their passion before they awoke fully.

He slept deeply then, resting his head on Hannah's soft breasts.

The scent of her skin eased his pain. Her hands smoothed his hair, his shoulders; she kissed the scar, following the shape with soft lips. Using his last bit of strength, Dan tried to ease his heavy weight away. "I'm too heavy...."

"Shh. You're not going anywhere." Hannah held him as though she would never let go.

Dan awoke slowly, searching across the rumpled sheets for Hannah. Fear shot through him, taking him to his feet, his heart pounding. "Hannah!"

Galahad began barking, bounding across the bed and sliding on the floors. He grinned up at Dan; the scrap of Hannah's torn lace briefs dangled from his teeth. After fighting the puppy for the scrap, Dan crushed the lace in his fist and tried to steady his rapid heartbeat.

A sewing machine in the living room hummed. The smell of bacon and coffee curled up to tantalize him. Else's husky tones joined Hannah's as they laughed outright.

In a burst of genius, Galahad ripped the briefs from Dan's fist and ran downstairs, dropping them at Else's feet. She lifted an eyebrow and stared coolly up the stairs while Hannah swished the briefs into her jeans pocket. "Hmm," Else said, grinning up at Dan. "You've changed since I diapered you...."

When Dan's blush faded and jeans sheathed his aroused body, he returned down the stairs. "Who invited you, Else?" he asked roughly, at odds with the joy bubbling inside him and the need to be alone with Hannah.

Else patted his cheek and handed him a cup of coffee. "Hannah did. We're sewing. Go away. Build a fence or something. Serves you right for worrying everyone."

Dan stared at Hannah, trying to speak when words would not come. Her hair tumbled around her shoulders, glinting fire, and her eyes filled with him.

Else disappeared and Dan blinked, waiting for Hannah to escape his reality. But she stood, cloth in hand and a tape measure curling around her neck.

"What are you doing?" he asked, trying to find his balance.

She smoothed his scar tenderly, kissing it. "Working. Do you always wake up charging around the house and yelling?"

"Come here." He dragged her against him, lifting her high against him. She smelled of soap, her hair damp against his face. "It was real, wasn't it?" he asked shakily, noting the faint bruise on her throat and the scrape marks of his beard.

"Real enough. I should have shot you instead . . . making everyone worry about you.... Shame on you."

Then she smiled tenderly and Dan forgot everything but the sweet kiss that followed.

Hannah worked long days at his house, spending the nights between the ranches. She reserved weekends for the Camelot, plowing unused land and easing the past.

Dan waited, savored the scents she left behind as the house began to take shape, and cursed the will that kept them apart. He'd asked her to bend once; his fire woman would have to take the next step in their fandango.

He shuffled through the small stack of receipts, replacing the cash, which he insisted she use. Minor purchases—

kitchen pots, bath towels, thread and fabrics, practical stainless-steel utensils—mingled with canvas, tubes of oil paint and brushes.

He noted the sprawling light colors and clean Western lines in the living room. The rugs, vases, trunks and furniture he'd hoarded for years had been put to good use. Hannah's large textured painting in light ochres, browns and creams filled an empty wall with delicate color. Dan studied the bold sweeps and rough textures, the impression of space and time soaring across the canvas. Hannah was like that—free, timeless brush strokes of little-girl excitement and the heady, mysterious taste of a woman.

Would Hannah leave or stay?

Without her near him, Dan awoke in the sweat of his nightmares.

In the flash of sun on a blue-black raven's wing, his dream could fly away.

Eleven

Spring drifted over the mountains in shades of green, while patches of wildflowers caught the May mist. A reminder of Earl, Macedonia quietly passed away one night, taking with him a portion of Hannah's guilty burden.

Galahad chased jackrabbits and stayed away from Big Al, who continued to love Hannah, despite her straying heart.

Dan grew more fascinating in every way. He protested a day spent prowling through flea markets, away from his cattle who approached calving. The Blaylocks swung into action, ordering Dan off both ranches while they tended the herds. At the end of the day, laden with pottery, antique jars and some cowboy's rusty forgotten left spur, Dan pulled out a rakish, boyish grin that sank Hannah's heart.

They had pulled into a pine bower, made love in the front seat of her pickup, and Big Al snorted his displeasure in the spring night. Dan had eased from Hannah's arms with a curse, stepped to the rocks with his bare feet. He had stood in the moonlight, head back, hands on hips, a strong man dressed only in his curses. Big Al pawed the freshly plowed earth and snorted. Hannah laughed as the males confronted each other and Dan began picking his way painfully back to the pickup. Before he could growl and snap, Hannah dragged him back in.

She enjoyed tending Dan's ruffled pride, teasing and tormenting, watching his expressions change. Then Dan's lovemaking began again....

Now Hannah drove by the field she had plowed on the first Saturday of May, inhaling the dark, rich scents of the earth. She passed Earl's prime cow nursing a new "beefalo" calf and everything in her turned soft and warm.

Determined to finish Dan's house and build a steady income, she'd taken small telephone consulting jobs for Ethan. Pleased with the way their styles remained compatible, she began depositing regular amounts in the account to repay Dan.

She ran her hand, callused now, across Jessie's scarred steering wheel. She'd fought the land for years and now she was back.

Valuing Dan's expert advice, she planned to grow hay and alfalfa, building an account at the feed store. She glanced back at the calf, nudging his mother's side. Hannah had forgotten how sweet new life was, how the land opened hurts and healed them in the spring.

She'd found her place, bartering her skills for those of the neighbors, and feeling richer every day. Earl's dream of a beautiful, productive Camelot shimmered within reach. The house, though comfortable, had to wait. By October, she intended to place a hefty payment against the major amounts Dan had wedged into saving the ranch.

When she made her final commitments, she wanted everything clear between them—her guilt resolved or tempered and controlled. She wanted the debt to Dan eased, repaying him by decorating and with money. Then she wanted to know that she could hold her land.

Apache whinnied and pranced as she passed, his mottled coat gleaming in the morning sun. When the Jasmine Annual Race came in late June, Apache's strength would far outdistance the other horses entered in the first event—a short, fast, dangerous race. Filled with males, the course had never been ridden by a woman, but Hannah intended to enter and win.

The racecourse skirted around a small hill, dipping and cornering through stands of trees. A dangerous rise, requiring a strong horse and stronger rider, lay just before the finish line. The merchants backed the race with a trophy and a fat check that Hannah wanted badly.

The second event, with more prize money, consisted of the same course, a relay of horses and added a long, straight race to the finish. Apache's Appaloosa strain could compete in the first stage, but he had little chance to finish first in the long endurance ride. Hannah entered the second event, and began searching for a likely horse.

She tapped her leather glove on her denim-clad knee. Torn and mended, her designer jeans had well served their purpose, wearing on her comfortably as did the land.

Steering into the Flying H spread on Monday morning, Hannah noted the small garden Dan had begun in the back.

Dan. Edgy at times, tender and passionate, he slid back into her mind.

Bred to the land, Dan wore his masculinity well. Little girls found him irresistible and he returned the favor. Big girls looked a second time as he passed.

He noticed every small change, adding his thoughts to her ideas about the house. There was a sweet, fierce desperation in his lovemaking now, yet he shielded a part of him from her.

Hannah backed the pickup to his front porch, eager to see his response to the massive bench table. Covered with a canvas tarp and laden with tools, the Andersons' eighty-year-old fruitwood table suited Dan's kitchen.

Though it was almost noon, Dan's pickup stood in the drive and Galahad wasn't running out the door. Hannah frowned, scanning the ranch yard for Dan, then ripped off her gloves. Just as her hand touched the brass doorknob, the door opened and a young woman with huge tear-filled eyes stared up at her.

Blond curls tumbled around a beautiful, faintly familiar face. Petite and curvy beneath the tattered flannel robe, the woman tried to smile. She failed, blowing her nose on a crumpled tissue and managing, "Dan and I are busy now. But you can come in."

"Melissa? Who is it?" Dan asked from the shadows of his office. Then he was striding toward Hannah in his bare feet, his bearded face taut and grim. Hanging loose on his chest, his wrinkled shirt barely covered the dark hair she loved to touch.

His hand shackled her wrist, his other running through his hair until it stood in peaks. He jerked her into the house and slammed the door; his jaw locked in a familiar gesture of iron will. "This is not what it looks like," he muttered, glancing at Melissa's robe fluttering as she flew back to his office.

Clearly Dan expected Hannah to start swinging at any moment, because he took her other wrist. "You are going to listen until I'm finished, damn it," he commanded in a no-nonsense lordly tone.

She grinned up at him, finding him totally distracting and appealing as he fought for control. "Go on. Explain away."

"I love you. Always have. That's what is important to remember now, Hannah. You let loose that fiery temper and we're both in trouble. You've got to remember that appearances aren't always what they seem. That if you run off, I'll come after you this time and tie you to the bed until you realize that nothing has happened." He breathed deeply, his morning scents of soap and coffee mingling, tantalizing her senses.

Frustrated and obviously fighting to say the right words to her, Dan finished with a harsh statement. "You've got to trust me. Melissa and I . . . we're not—"

He stopped when Hannah's lips absorbed his unspoken words. She leaned her head against his chest and smoothed the hair covering his chest. Fluttering her lashes against his throat, Hannah smiled as Dan's tense body shuddered. "What's little old Dan been doing?" she cooed.

"This isn't funny," he snapped as she cuddled closer. "I want you to know—"

The flick of her tongue across his nipple made him catch his breath. She smoothed his cheek, loving the feel of his beard against her palm. He was clearly frightened, remembering the scene that caused her flight years ago. "I trust you, Dan."

He shifted his weight restlessly, examining her face closely just as Melissa sobbed loudly. "We're watching soaps," he admitted slowly, as if the words were dragged out of him. "I tutor Melissa in Western roles, and she hates horses and cows. We started watching soaps as a trade-off.... Fiona has just returned to Rex, her first husband. You're making me miss the good part. Mindy isn't taping for me today—"

"What are we waiting for?" She jumped into his arms, delighted by the easy strength that carried her into his office. Dan sank into an overstuffed armchair with her, while Melissa sobbed quietly on the floor, amid a growing stack of crumpled tissues.

"Sit still," Dan ordered, when Hannah wiggled on his lap. "You're distracting me. You always do. You always have," he admitted in an absent tone, just as Fiona and Rex kissed on-screen.

"Poor baby," she returned, curling her arm around his shoulders. He almost jumped out of the chair when Fiona was caught in Fred's rumpled bed and the tip of Hannah's tongue flicked his ear.

The last week of June, Dan knew two things: the amount needed to redecorate his home was far beneath expectations and Hannah had signed to ride the dual murderous Jasmine Annual Races.

He crushed the list of riders in his leather glove as he stalked into the ice-cream parlor where Gordy Whipplecord was building Hannah a banana split. He placed one hand on the back of Hannah's neck, wanting to shake some sense into her, and tossed the crumpled paper to the counter. "Take Hannah's name off, Gordy. She isn't riding in either event."

The brilliant smile washing Hannah's face vanished, replaced by a frown. "Of course, I am. I've paid the entry fee. Apache and I are up to the race and we're riding in it." She tried to stand, but Dan's hand held her to the stool.

"No woman has ever ridden in that race," Dan stated from between the set line of his teeth.

"There's no rules to keep her from it," Gordy said mildly, while dropping a maraschino cherry on top of a mound of whipped cream. "She just needs a second horse for the big race."

"I will ride—" Hannah began, fighting the urge to break something—preferably the man holding her neck as though she were a scruffy, disobedient puppy.

Dan slashed a dark glare at her from beneath the shadows of his hat. His jaw flexed, the scar sliding across his tense muscle. "Damned if you will... She withdraws, Gordy."

"Have to hear it from the lady, Dan," Gordy returned, artistically sprinkling nuts over the banana split. "Where do you want this, Miss Hannah?"

"I'll give you one guess." While Hannah debated dumping the bowl of ice cream and toppings over Dan, or just shooting the can of whipped cream into the waist of his jeans, he plucked her out of her chair. Tossed across his shoulder, Hannah glimpsed down Dan's flat backside and legs to his dusty boots. She tried to catch her breath as they passed Else.

"'Morning, Else," Dan said grimly, lifting a glove from Hannah's buttocks to tip his hat to his sister. "Butt out," he added firmly, carrying Hannah to Apache and plopping her into the saddle.

In the next second, Hannah had jerked the light hitch free and Apache was tearing over the horse path that bordered Jasmine. Dan, crouching low in the saddle on Durango, followed.

"Oh, man. Trouble with a capital *T*," Roman Blaylock murmured, lifting his hat to Else as she came to stand beside him. They watched Dan's fast Arabian stallion covering the distance Apache had put between them. Dust flew from the hooves of the horses, Hannah's lean body bent low against the wind.

"When Miss Hannah is around, she stirs him up. Dan needs that," Else said after a moment. "Blaylock men get moldy when they're not stirred up. Did you get that cradle for Dan's babies done yet?"

Dan leaned forward, giving Durango his lead and cursing as a clod of dirt thrown by Apache's hooves soared by. "She can ride," he said to Durango, pushing the horse to his limits. The Arabian, bred for endurance, struggled in the Appaloosa's wake.

Bent forward, one hand holding Apache's reins loosely and her other hand opened on his strong shoulders, Hannah glanced back at Dan.

He read the anger and fear in her expression. Saw the fierce determination to win in the tense set of her body, straining to match the powerful horse. To Dan, the race represented her flight years ago. This time she'd listen to reason.

A race against the past and the future, the horses sensed the humans struggling, jockeying for power and surged over the rolling landscape, passing fir and pine in a blur. Hannah carried his heart, his life, riding across land their families had settled.

Hannah's hair caught fire, whipped by the wind. She glanced back again, tears streaming down her face.

Pushing for the next quarter mile, Durango began to overtake the Appaloosa's tiring hooves.

They soared over a small rise and Hannah began slowing Apache, talking to him. The horse was spent, sweating, straining for more and too exhausted to give her the freedom she wanted so desperately.

Nervous as his breed, Durango sidestepped just as Dan reached out to grab Apache's reins. "Back off," Hannah cried, tears sweeping trails down her dirty face.

"The hell I will," Dan returned, slowing Durango who had just hit his stride.

Apache breathed heavily, Hannah's hand patting him as she pressed white lips together grimly. "He's tired and needs cooling off. But if you think that I'm any less angry, you are dead wrong, Blaylock. You strutted into Whipplecord's and started tossing out orders about me like you always do. To top that, you hauled me out of there like a wayward child. Take that hand off my reins!''

"I ought to put it on your backside. You're pushing that horse just as hard as you do yourself." Then with a quick curse, he opened his hand and forced it away from Apache's reins. Hannah touched off a protective streak a mile wide in him, but this time she was right. He stayed Durango's need to race, pacing him to stay even with Apache.

Hannah's head was high, tears rolling down her cheeks to stain her dark blue cotton blouse. "You're on Ferguson land now, Blaylock," she said, looking straight ahead.

"So I am. Make no lines between us, Smokey. Because you're mine and always will be."

She shot him a look of sheer, hot defiance. "You stop ordering me around, Blaylock. I'm not your baby sister or your wife."

The horses' pace slowed, settling into a walk.

Dan reached to lock his fingers around her wrist, needing to hold her, to stay the fear squeezing his heart. "Listen to reason, Hannah. That race is barred to novices. One fall and you could end up in the Ferguson family cemetery plot."

She lifted her head and a fiery tendril ignited in the sunlight. "You've run in both races."

Dan stroked the back of her hand with his thumb. "Not this year. I've got too much to live for now. Now that this ranch business is out of the way—"

"Out of the way?" Hannah's brows lifted, her fingers tightening on Apache's reins. "What makes you think it is? Did you decide that, too?"

She flushed under Dan's hard look, but held the stare.

Taking a deep breath and tossing caution away, Dan said, "You sleep on your couch when you're not with me. Why?"

Hannah turned away, a muscle sliding in her slender throat as she swallowed. "That's my business."

"You can't sleep any better away from me than I can from you. You kill yourself in that damn race and we'll both be sleeping away from each other permanently."

Hannah jerked her hand away, placing her fingers flat on her thigh as they continued walking the horses. "Don't push me, Dan," she said quietly, noting Big Al's buffalo herd grazing in a lush field. "I'm riding."

He rubbed his fingers on his thigh, rubbing away the feel of slender bones and soft flesh. "You're pushing yourself by running this place and working at mine. I don't want you killing yourself out of gratitude to me or to repay—the hell with the ranches. Earl wanted you back and so did I. He didn't want you to die filling his dreams."

Dan took a deep breath and pushed out the words, "I came after you once in Seattle, saw you kiss your...Jordan, and I died. I pushed hard because part of me ripped away at that kiss. Sure, I wanted to hurt you, drive you into hurting the way—"

"You think I don't hurt?" Hannah slashed the back of her hand across her face. "What do you think all this is about, Dan? Gratitude? Sex? What?"

Pain went streaking through him, an ache to hold her so strong it hurt. Instinct told him to drive to the bone, making a clean cut and healing it later. "You're not charging me full price on the house. Why not? You think I can't handle it?"

Her eyes flickered. "I pay my debts."

Part of him bled. Another part hoped. "That's all there is between us? Mortgages, gratitude and sex?"

For an instant Hannah's smoky eyes darkened. Dan's blood stopped flowing as he waited, his throat dry. "There's trust. You'll have to trust me about the house. And the race."

He'd hoped for more, needing a commitment from her more desperately than air. Durango sidestepped nervously, sensing the tension racing through Dan.

"That's a lot of trust," he said, staring at Big Al who began sauntering toward the fence. As the horses walked, Dan rubbed his sweaty hand on his jeans, then strangled the reins again. If that was all Hannah wanted to say—

"Then there's more," she said softly, her fingers sliding through his. "There's love, Dan. Love, deep and rich, filling me. I've found what I've needed all these years and I want to come to you free of guilt and broken pride."

"Think so?" he asked unevenly a moment later, sunlight catching the tears dancing on his lashes. "Kill yourself and we won't have that chance."

The sunlight and shadows passed between them before Hannah halted Apache. "I'm doing this my way, Dan. Then we'll be free. The house is my gift to you and I enjoyed every minute of seeing its beauty come to life. You've given to me, and now I need to give to you...."

He slid to the ground, reaching for her and holding her close. After a moment, he brushed a bit of dust from her cheek and kissed the spot. "You're telling me that this love thing is a two-way street, hmm?"

Holding him tightly, Hannah gently bit his neck. "Think you're up to it, Blaylock?"

Suddenly Dan was young and filled with life, stepping into the sunshine and shedding the past. "Think so. There's one condition to my serious intentions—that you let me help you practice and that you ride Durango in the second race."

She stared at him, then brushed away a fleck of dirt from his scar and grinned. "What a guy. Knows he's down for the count and still trying to set conditions. You start wearing your glasses when I'm around and we'll bargain—"

For a minute, Dan glared at her, trying for a suitable comeback. Her kiss made him forget everything but the soft, sweet swell of love washing over him.

Logan nudged Dan with his shoulder as the horses lined up for the first race in the morning. "She'll do," he said quietly, as Hannah adjusted her body to the saddle, wearing the long-sleeved shirt Dan had suggested.

"Women," Dan muttered, strangling the locket Hannah had thrust into his hands at the last-minute kiss.

"Best damn game in town," Logan returned easily.

"Contrary, moody—"

"Sweet. Soft. Make us feel like giants striding across volcanoes—"

"Mule-headed—" A horse leaped forward, a false start, and had to be settled back in line. Hannah talked quietly to Apache, her hair gathered back by a rubber band. She forced her concentration to the race, calming the Appaloosa who stamped impatiently.

"Silk and satin. I bet you're thinking about how you'd like to rip her off Apache's saddle right now, little brother. Miss Hannah would just claw her way back."

"Give her the lead and she'll run with it...." Dan muttered, ignoring Logan's quick roar of laughter. "Headstrong—"

The pistol shot stopped his heart as the horses surged forward. The only woman in the race, Hannah's light weight was an advantage as Apache quickly took the lead into a rise that plummeted into a shallow stream.

Focused on the race, Dan nodded to the flying rhythm of the twenty-seven horses' hooves. "Take the inside...take the inside, Smokey, talk to him...talk to him."

Logan glanced at Dan. "Don't know why, but Miss Hannah loves you."

"Damn right, she does," Dan tossed back, not missing a beat.

"Must have cost you...letting her ride today," Logan pushed.

"Letting her," Dan repeated dryly, his eyes pinned to Hannah and Apache. "She's her own woman."

"I was wondering when you would understand," Logan murmured. "Miss Hannah can't be pushed."

A rider whipped his horse close to Apache and Hannah reached out, snagged the whip and threw it aside. The other rider yelled something and Dan tensed, his chest tight as Hannah concentrated on bending low, keeping her knees tight against Apache's belly.

Dan made a mental note that Harlan Thomsen was due a black eye.

The horses dropped over the rise and one rolled down the steep drop to the stream. The rider scrambled to safety as another horse went down. Taking the lead, Hannah leaned back to balance Apache as he picked his way down the dirt and rock course.

Three more horses went down in the water and one more failed the opposite incline. With four other riders, Hannah took the lead of the pack and Dan forgot to breathe.

"You'll name the first baby after Mother if it's a girl and after me if it's a boy, right?" Logan asked, as the riders swooped around the tree marking the end of the course.

"Uh-huh." Dan brought the locket to his mouth, kissing it. "Do it, baby. Do it. Ride like hell now and give Apache time to take that stream."

Hannah leaned low in the saddle, talking to Apache when he topped the ridge preceding the short stretch to the finish line. Loving her, the horse fought his limits, and Dan understood. Riding his fear and realizing that Hannah needed this race for her pride, Dan fought twin battles.

"Whew." Logan leaned forward with Dan as Hannah led the race. "She's got the race. There's only one person I've ever seen become a part of the horse like that—you, Dan."

But Dan was running to the winner's circle. "Get someone to cool down Apache," he ordered over his shoulder.

Then Hannah was laughing, crying, holding him tight as she slid into his arms. "I won! Oh, Dan, I won!"

Late in the afternoon the second event loomed ahead and Dan's stomach began to lurch. Durango knew Hannah well, but his nervous blood could make the difference when racing with other horses. Hannah tended Dan's battered emotions with a strawberry-flavored-snowcone kiss. Before he lifted her to Apache's saddle, she stroked his cheek and held him tight, despite the hoard of Blaylocks grinning behind her. Big Al and El Capitan, honorees of the celebration, looked on the milling crowd with kingly disdain.

"Wear this for luck," Dan said suddenly, thrusting his mother's wedding band on Hannah's hand. "And remember that Durango needs plenty of rein. Watch out for

Johnny Vasquez—he rides close and Durango doesn't like it."

"Vasquez will eat our dust," Hannah promised promptly, studying the ring on her finger and glowing up at him. "Thank you, Dan."

"Love me instead," he returned, raising for her last kiss.

"Always have," she returned against his lips.

Apache took the lead immediately while Dan held Durango ready for Hannah. Then she was crossing horses, transferring to Durango while running with Apache.

The crowd cheered, but Dan heard only his heart beating, hurting, filling his chest as he watched. If Durango went down... If the saddle cinch broke... If another rider... Dan fought to keep his stomach down, his face and body were damp with sweat as Durango stretched out for the race to the finish line.

It hurt to let her go, but the wound healed by her growing love. He'd wanted her wrapped in safety, tucked at his side. Hannah couldn't be molded into the aproned housewife of his dreams; she wanted a partnership that would be difficult for him to yield.

"To keep Hannah, I will," he swore quietly, watching Arabian and woman skim across the horizon. Hannah bent low, one hand on the reins and the other splayed on Durango's strong neck. She was talking to him, letting him feel her desperation, her pride.

"Give him more rein," Dan whispered across dry lips. Then tail high, Durango swept toward the finish line and Dan began running toward Hannah. She broke the winner's ribbon and continued to run Durango around the track, talking to him while she sought out Dan.

Her eyes locked on Dan, keeping him still. Hannah smiled and talked as she cooled the horse, bringing him down to walking. Durango carried her to Dan and stopped. Sunlight burned a fiery red halo around her hair, her gray eyes dark as a stormy night, her head held high with pride.

Time skipped by as emotions cut Dan away from the noise of the crowd. *He'd loved her for years and now his fire woman had come for him.* Hannah met Dan's eyes, her head high.

"I've found my place. This is where I belong. In October, I'll move into your place. Not before. I want to finish the year. Earl's buffalo herd will stay in the wild, the way he wanted."

While Dan reeled with her statement, reaching for her, Hannah glanced at the approaching crowd and closed her eyes. "I love you, Daniel Josiah Blaylock. Get me out of here."

Then she was in his arms, drained and needing him. Dan shuddered, unashamed of the tears burning his eyes. He carried her to a small house used by visiting celebrities and locked the door.

Hannah was his, a part of his heart, soft and yielding against him. Her eyes watched him, darkened with love, as he lifted her chin for his kiss. "Make love to me, Dan," she whispered as he stroked the damp hair away from her cheek. "Make love to me forever."

"Miss Hannah, it would be a pleasure to make love with you," he answered in true courtly Blaylock manner.

Big Al snorted outside the house, bumping the walls pleasantly with his two-thousand-pound frame. The Blaylock brothers led a wagon train, circling the house with horseback riders and shooting off starting pistols. El Capitan bellowed and broke through a wooden fence, headed for the open range. The band began playing at sunset for the open-air dance.

Inside the house, Dan and Hannah touched and held, renewing their love as though the entire world were soft and quiet and created just for the two of them.

Epilogue

Almost a year later, Dan stood near his mother's loom, watching his wife complete a wall hanging for their bedroom. Tiny and precious, Delilah Elizabeth Blaylock cuddled against his shoulder and Dan tenderly kissed her fiery cap of curls. Hannah's and his love had circled the years, binding them together with a child and fulfilling his happiness. His fascination with Hannah deepened every minute. He'd learned to test the mysterious feminine waters before issuing a high-handed command that ultimately left her defensive. Hannah's pregnancy occurred immediately after a medical procedure and Dan found himself struggling with feminine mental mazes. They clashed inevitably, drawn closer by exploring each other's limits.

Progress on the Ferguson homestead was temporarily halted, due to Delilah's birth. Finally at peace with her past, Hannah intended to keep the home dear to her.

Dan tried placing aside the fear nagging at his happiness, and found himself speaking it aloud. "Don't even think about riding in the race. Delilah is only two weeks old and you're a nursing mother.''

Hannah stopped weaving, rising slowly to slide into Dan's free arm. ''Stop growling. My only serious intentions run more to getting back in shape.'' She kissed the taut side of his neck, blinking her eyelashes against his dark skin. ''Daniel Josiah. You take a lot of tending and love. In fact, you've done so well this year, staying those macho tendencies, that I've decided to recover your favorite chair and try for another baby.''

His eyebrows soared, black eyes gleaming down at her with pleasure as he locked her to his side. ''Think so?''

Hannah's lips brushed his, her eyes filled with love. ''Oh, yes. Truly, I do.''

*   *   *   *   *

BIG SUMMER READ

Summer Reading At Its Best

In July, Harlequin and Silhouette bring readers the Big Summer Read Program. Heat up your summer with these four exciting new novels by top Harlequin and Silhouette authors.

SOMEWHERE IN TIME by Barbara Bretton
YESTERDAY COMES TOMORROW by Rebecca Flanders
A DAY IN APRIL by Mary Lynn Baxter
LOVE CHILD by Patricia Coughlin

From time travel to fame and fortune, this program offers something for everyone.

Available at your favorite retail outlet.

BSR

SILHOUETTE® Desire™

MAN OF THE MONTH

**YOU'VE ASKED FOR IT,
YOU'VE GOT IT!
MAN OF THE MONTH: 1992**

ONLY FROM SILHOUETTE DESIRE

You just couldn't get enough of them, those men from Silhouette Desire—twelve sinfully sexy, delightfully devilish heroes. Some will make you sweat, some will make you sigh . . . but every long, lean one of them will have you swooning. So here they are, *more* of the men we couldn't resist bringing to you for one more year. . . .

BEST MAN FOR THE JOB
by Dixie Browning in June

MIDNIGHT RIDER
by Cait London in July

CONVENIENT HUSBAND
by Joan Hohl in August

NAVARRONE
by Helen R. Myers in September

A MAN OF HONOR
by Paula Detmer Riggs in October

BLUE SKY GUY
by Carole Buck in November

IT HAD TO BE YOU
by Jennifer Greene in December

Don't let these men get away! MAN OF THE MONTH, only in Silhouette Desire!

MOM92JD

Celebrate with a FREE classic collection of romance!

In honor of its 10th anniversary, Silhouette Desire has a gift for you! A limited edition, hardcover anthology of three early Silhouette Desire titles, written by three of your favorite authors:

> **DIANA PALMER**—*September Morning*
> **JENNIFER GREENE**—*Body and Soul*
> **LASS SMALL**—*To Meet Again*

This unique collection will not be available in retail stores and is only available through this exclusive offer.

Send your name, address and zip or postal code, along with six proof-of-purchase coupons from any Silhouette Desire published in June, July or August, plus $2.75 for postage and handling (check or money order—please do not send cash) payable to Silhouette Books, to:

In the U.S.	In Canada
Desire 10th Anniversary	Desire 10th Anniversary
Silhouette Books	Silhouette Books
3010 Walden Avenue	P.O. Box 609
P.O. Box 9057	Fort Erie, Ontario
Buffalo, NY 14269-9057	L2A 5X3

(Please allow 4-6 weeks for delivery. Hurry! Quantities are limited. Offer expires September 30, 1992.)   SDANPOP-R

SILHOUETTE DESIRE
10TH ANNIVERSARY
proof-of-purchase